This book belongs to

_____

Children's
POOLBEG

Spike and the Professor

First published 1989 by
Poolbeg Press Ltd
Knocksedan House,
Swords, Co Dublin, Ireland

Reprinted January 1991
Reprinted May 1995

© Tony Hickey 1989

Poolbeg Press receives financial assistance from The
Arts Council, An Chomhairle Ealaíon, Ireland

ISBN 1 85371 039 3

Cover design by Robert Ballagh
Illustrations by Robert Ballagh
Printed by The Guernsey Press Co Ltd,
Vale, Guernsey, Channel Islands.

Spike and the Professor

Tony Hickey

Children's
POOLBEG

Tony Hickey was born in Newbridge, Co. Kildare and lived there until his family moved to Dublin when he was fourteen years old. He has worked extensively in radio and television, with many successful dramatisations of adult and children's works to his credit.

For Kate and Denis

Doreen

Chapter One

pike and the Professor were the very best of friends. Yet it was hard to imagine two boys more different from each other.

Spike was tall for his age, which was ten, and lived in Irishtown, once a separate village from Dublin but now part of the city. His real name was Stephen Arthur Patrick O'Halligan and he owed his nickname to a piece of hair which, when he was little, always stood up no matter how hard his mother tried to comb it flat. A visiting uncle from London had said, "Stephen Arthur looks as though he has a spike on the back of his head." The nickname continued to be used long after Stephen Arthur's hair had been partially tamed and flattened by Mr Riley, the local barber.

The Professor, although the same age as

Spike, was smaller with light-brown hair. He owed his nickname to several things. First, there were the heavy horn-rimmed glasses that he always wore. Secondly, his father was actually a professor. Thirdly, and, perhaps, most important, one day while he was writing an essay, he didn't hear Mr Brannigan, the teacher, say "Time up." Finally, Mr Brannigan had to tap him on the shoulder and say, "Hey, professor, you're not writing a book."

The rest of the class, which included Spike, had laughed but the Professor (real name Damien Hayden O'Neill) hadn't minded in the least. Being given a nickname somehow made him feel as though he belonged in the school for he and his family had only just moved into Sandymount, the area next to Irishtown, and he knew almost no-one in the district.

In fact, some of the other boys had ganged up against him because his father was a university professor. Worse again, his mother reviewed books for one of the daily papers.

Many people, both pupils and parents, thought it strange that the Professor should go to the local school at all. They thought he'd be more at home in one of the expensive fee-paying places.

Spike's mother felt this way. "He'd be better

off among his own kind," she said one day at dinner-time when her daughter, Doreen, mentioned seeing the Professor.

"And if he was among his own kind," her husband said, "you'd be accusing his father and mother of being snobs."

"I wouldn't have to accuse them of anything at all for I wouldn't ever have heard of them," Mrs. O'Halligan said. And this in a way was true for there was very little contact between the residents of Sandymount and those of Irishtown. Many Irishtown people regarded themselves as special because their families had lived there for generations. Newcomers were often regarded with suspicion and none more so than those who had recently moved into Dublin 4, which, for no apparent reason that the residents of Dublin 4 (Sandymount) could discover, was regarded as an area of great wealth and privilege.

"They're just workers like you and me," Spike's father said, which Spike thought was odd since his father had been out of work for the last six months.

"Workers me foot," Spike's mother snapped. "They've never got their hands dirty in their entire lives."

Spike wanted to say that maybe it was a

nice thing not to have to get your hands dirty. But then maybe his mother would think that was an odd thing for him to say since, no matter how careful he was, he always ended up with black fingernails and filthy hands. So, instead of joining in his parents' conversation and maybe getting into trouble, he slipped out of the house to see if there was anyone playing football on the grass or outlaws on the mound, which had once been the city dump and now has lovely little houses built on and around it. The part nearest the Pidgeon House had become a great recreation area for people of all ages.

He hadn't gone very far when he saw the Professor strolling along one of the pathways all by himself. The Professor looked so lonely that Spike decided to speak to him. "Hi 'ya. What are you doing here?"

"Just exploring."

"By yourself?"

The Professor nodded.

"Have you no mates to knock around with?"

"My mates are all in Cork. That's where we used to live."

"Is that why you talk funny? Because you're from Cork?"

"Maybe." Then the Professor grinned. "I

think you talk funny too but maybe that's because you're from Dublin."

Spike grinned back. He liked a fellow who could take a joke. Better again, he liked a fellow who could turn a joke around without being nasty. He said, "You can't go back to Cork every time you want someone to knock around with. Are there no lads on your road?"

The Professor said, "they're either too young or too old. The only people my age are all girls. Even if I wanted to, they wouldn't let me knock around with them."

"I have the opposite problem," Spike said. "I have a sister, Doreen, who's a year younger than me. She'd follow me day and night if I let her."

This wasn't exactly true. Doreen only followed Spike when she had nothing better to do or when she thought that Spike was up to something interesting. Fortunately that afternoon she was doing the shopping for their granny; a task which Spike and she took turns to perform.

"I'll show you around if you like," Spike said. "Would you like to see where I live?"

The Professor was very impressed by the outside of Spike's house. "Can we go in?"

"Of course we can," Spike said.

Mrs O'Halligan was by herself in the kitchen. "Who's this then?" Her voice showed that she was still feeling cross with her husband for disagreeing with her about what was real work.

"It's the Professor. He's from Cork. He wanted to see the inside of the house."

"Oh really? Do they not have houses in Cork then?"

The Professor thought Mrs O'Halligan was making a joke. "Of course they do. But not like this."

"Oh, and what's so different about this one?"

"It's like a house in a film," the Professor said.

Neither Spike nor his mother knew what to make of this reply. Spike, however, decided to take no chances on his mother becoming more cross. He moved towards the door.

His mother, however, was not willing to let the conversation end. "I've heard of you before," she said to the Professor. "In fact, Spike's father and me were discussing you just before he went out. We were wondering why you were at Spike's school."

"My father thinks it's good for me," the Professor said.

Spike and his mother didn't know what to

make of this reply either. And this time Spike, in spite of the need to be careful about how the conversation might go, allowed his curiosity to get the better of him. "What does your father mean by 'good?' Are not all schools supposed to be good for you?"

"Father thinks I should have a wide experience of life."

"In other words, see how the other half lives," Mrs O'Halligan's jaw tightened. "Including looking at the inside of their houses. Then you go home to you own grand house and report on what you find out."

The Professor suddenly realised that Mrs. O'Halligan wasn't making any kind of joke. He blushed and stammered slightly. "Oh no, it's not like that at all."

Mrs O'Halligan's firm expression relaxed somewhat as she saw that the Professor was both sincere and upset. "Maybe not as far as you're concerned but that's not to say that we all feel the same about such things."

Spike decided it was definitely time to leave. "We'll cut down through Ringsend and look at the river," he said.

"Don't be late for your tea," his mother said, although it was only half-past two.

"I won't."

The two boys stepped out into the bright afternoon. Traffic droned by

"I didn't mean to upset her," the Professor said.

"Oh, don't blame yourself. She often gets that way for no reason at all." A sudden thought came to Spike. "It's been like that ever since Dad's been out of work. She worries a lot."

"My mother was the same for a while."

Spike stared, amazed, at the Professor. "Your Dad was out of work too?"

"Yes, while he was waiting to hear if he'd got his present job in Dublin."

"But you live in a huge house."

"It's not that big. It just seems big because of the windows and the garden around it. You can come and have a look at it tomorrow if you like."

"Great," Spike said, deciding at the same time not to mention the invitation to his mother until after the visit. "What did you mean when you said our house was like something out of a film?"

The Professor began to blush again. "I just meant that it looked kind of... of old."

"Well it is old. Most things around here are old. The Protestant church on the main road is well over two hundred years old. People have lived around here since the city began. Did you ever see a map of old Dublin?"

"No," the Professor said.

"There's one in a book in the library. Do you ever go to the library?"

"No, but I love reading."

"So do I. We'll go when we finish the tour."

And so that meeting on the mound became the first of many such outings. Spike found he enjoyed showing the Professor around Ringsend and Irishtown and passing on the stories he had heard from his grandmother about the days when Ringsend had been a great fishing harbour with its own shipyards, which everyone hoped would start again.

He took him as far as the lighthouse past Costelloe's Fort and told him the story of how that got its name.

Then they crossed over the canal lock by the river Dodder and looked at the beautiful tiles that covered the bottom of the docking area.

Once this had been one of the busiest shipping places in Ireland with coal boats coming from England.

The same was true of the quays that lined the mouth of the Liffey. Ships from all over the world used dock there: cargo and passenger ships. There had been a ferry as well that carried people across to the north side of the city. Now, with so many motor cars and the toll bridge, the ferry had gone out of business, and, instead of ships, small yachts and sailing boats bobbed up and down on the salt water.

By way of return for all this information, the Professor told Spike about Cork and its bridges and river and how boats could dock right up in the middle of the city. He told him about Kinsale as well and of the great forts close to it; real forts where real soldiers had been garrisoned.

He also kept his promise to take Spike to his house.

Spike at first was overawed by the amount of space in it. It was so bright as well, with doors that opened into a garden with fruit trees. "Maybe your mother would like some apples when they are ripe," Mrs O'Neill said.

Spike liked Mrs O'Neill once he got used to her. She was quite different from his own mother in the way that she spoke and dressed and behaved. She seemed to be so easy going. Yet everything was done the way she wanted it. Even the real Professor O'Neill, who was a sandy-coloured, blurred kind of man, given to scattering papers around the sitting room, always ended up tidying them away before Mrs O'Neill had to ask him.

Spike's mother sniffed a bit when she heard Spike had not only gone to the house but had been given tea and carrot cake. "Carrot cake? It'll be lettuce buns next, I suppose."

The real surprise in the O'Neill house, however, was the computer room with a print-out and a word processor and a graphics section.

"That's what my father is a professor of," the younger Professor explained. "Next year he's going to start to teach me how to use all this equipment. He'll probably let you learn too."

"That'd be great," Spike said.

Once school was finished and the summer holidays begun, Spike and the Professor began to explore the inner city. Often other boys went with them. Then the exploring would turn into a game of chase. Sometimes Doreen would tag along and, while the Professor thought she wasn't too bad, Spike wished she'd stay home.

And yet it was thanks to Doreen that they found out about the special day excursion to Cork and Kinsale.

She'd been following them down O'Connell Street when suddenly she paused in front of a travel agency and called out, "Hey, look! There's a special excursion next week to Cork and Kinsale. Children are half price."

Spike and the Professor studied the poster carefully. "It might as well be full price as far as I'm concerned," Spike finally said. "There's no way I can get that kind of money with Dad out of work, especially since Doreen might want to come as well."

"I have enough money in the post office right now to buy my ticket," Doreen declared. "I saved what I was given at my confirmation. I might even lend you some if you weren't so nasty to me all the time."

"Mam might not like you drawing it out," Spike said.

"Of course she won't mind. The money belongs to me."

"How much could you lend me?"

Doreen wrinkled her nose. "Well, if I was to agree to lend you anything at all, I suppose I could make it five pounds."

"I could lend you another three," the Professor said.

"That still leaves me seven pounds short," Spike sighed.

"You could try earning it, doing odd jobs," Doreen said.

"Those jobs have all been taken by the big lads. They wouldn't give me a look in. The only thing left is maybe running messages and Mam'd scalp me if she found out I was taking money from any of the old people. No, no. It's just hopeless unless, Doreen, you were to stay at home."

"And let you use my money to go instead? You must be joking. I wouldn't miss an outing like this for the world. I want to see all those places that the Professor has been talking about to you."

"I'd like to see them again too," the Professor said. "And Spike, you shouldn't be so negative in your outlook."

"And what does that mean when it's at home?" asked Spike.

"It means that you give up too easily. Doreen is right. You could try earning the money. The three of us could try earning it for you. All we have to do is think of a good idea."

Chapter Two

or the remainder of that day and for all of the next day, Spike and the Professor, and sometimes Doreen, sat and sat and thought and thought until Spike was sure his brain would boil. Yet no-one came up with a really good idea for earning money.

The Professor, for example, suggested that they put on a play. But there wasn't time to organise that. And anyway Spike couldn't quite see the other children in the neighbourhood coughing up seven pounds to see himself and the Professor and Doreen in a play, especially since Doreen said she'd have to be let wear her granny's short fur jacket and have as much to say and do as the two boys.

Then they thought of singing on street corners. But they didn't know enough songs.

Neither were they sure how that idea would go
down with their parents if someone they knew
recognised them singing in the centre of the
city, which seemed to be the only sensible
place in which to do it. Also the Professor's
singing sounded like a foghorn with stomach
ache.

"If only we'd found out about the excursion
earlier," Spike sighed as he and the Professor
walked along Londonbridge Road where new
drains were being laid. One side of the road
was completely up, causing a great delay to
cars and lorries. The two boys slowed down to
look into the deepest trench they'd ever seen.

"You could bury a horse standing up in
that," the Professor said. "That is, of course, if
it was dead and you wanted to bury it
standing up."

"You could bury almost anything standing
up and not just a horse," Spike replied. Then
he felt totally depressed that he and the
Professor were having such a stupid
conversation instead of finding a solution to
their problem.

A passing van blew its horn at a wobbling
cyclist.

"That's the mobile caterers," the Professor
said. "During the fine weather they sell

sandwiches near Baggot Street Bridge. That's the kind of thing we need to be doing."

"Yeh, but they wouldn't let us set up in competition to them any more than the big fellows would let us go around cleaning windows and cutting grass. It's almost dinnertime. I'll meet you at the Tower at half-past two."

"O.K."

The Professor hurried home, wondering if he could ask his parents to lend him the money so that Spike could go on the excursion but he wasn't sure how Spike's mother would feel about that. She was getting more and more sensitive about her husband not having a job. Mr O'Halligan was worried too. His eyes seemed sadder each time that the Professor saw him although he always tried to crack a joke. But his laughter was hollow.

"Well and what did you and Spike get up to today?" Mrs O'Neill asked as she watched her son wash his hands.

"Not much, just walked around a bit, talked about the excursion."

"You think he'll be able to go then, do you?"

"We have five more days to get it fixed up."

"I only hope all the tickets won't be sold."

Spike and the Professor had never even

considered such a terrible possibility. "Would they let us reserve them by 'phone?"

"Well they might but what would be the good if you couldn't pay for them?" Mrs O'Neill put a plate with a sliced tomato and a tuna-fish sandwich in front of her son. "That's all I had time to get ready. We can eat properly this evening when your father gets home."

"Spike and I were talking about sandwiches earlier on."

"Does he like them or hate them?"

"I don't know. We were talking about selling them rather than eating them. But it wasn't important."

"I see," Mrs O'Neill said.

"Are you not having anything to eat?" the Professor asked.

"What? No. It's too warm." Mrs O'Neill drifted out onto the patio. The chair by the window creaked as she sat on it and picked up the book she'd been reading. Once she got involved in that, nothing would disturb her until evening. That was why she'd had no time to prepare lunch.

The Professor ate the sandwich and then put the plate into the dishwasher. It was only a quarter past one. There was an hour and fifteen minutes before he was to meet Spike.

Maybe if he was to go for a walk by himself a brilliant idea would come to him.

He reached the corner of Pembroke Road and started towards Baggot Street but his mind remained blank. Now there was the added anxiety that the tickets might all be sold. If they were to put a deposit down and couldn't pay the full amount, they might end up losing that deposit.

The Professor sighed and then shivered, for suddenly the heat had gone out of the day. A sharp breeze scattered dust and litter. Clouds scudded across the sky. The leisurely aspect of the afternoon was suddenly gone. People hurried back to their offices before the rain began.

The Professor decided to make for the church in Haddington Road.

As he waited for the traffic lights to change, he saw the caterers' van. The owners, now that their customers had departed because of the change in the weather, were closing down.

The Professor reached the church door as the first of the huge raindrops bounced off the ground.

The church really was like a sanctuary from the downpour. In olden days people went to churches to escape arrest and imprisonment.

Or did only cathedrals have sanctuaries? But all churches had sanctuary lamps. He'd ask his father about that. Maybe he should ask his father about the seven pounds and how to earn it. Maybe now that he was in the church he should say a prayer about the matter.

"Dear God, help Spike and me to raise the seven pounds. That is, of course, if you want us to go on the day trip with Doreen to Cork and Kinsale."

That made the Professor feel much better. He genuflected and went out into the porch to see if the rain had stopped. The caterers' van passed, going towards Londonbridge Road. The rain began to ease off and in a few minutes stopped.

The Professor set off along the same route taken by the van. He dodged through the traffic that had become snarled up by the rain and ran under the railway bridge. Then he stopped, for only a few yards ahead there was what looked like a major drama, thrown into utter confusion by a crowd of onlookers, each of whom offered different versions of what had happened. But two things were absolutely undeniable. One was that the caterers' van was on its side in the recently dug trench. Secondly that a lorry, part of the pipe-laying activities, had ended up in a front garden.

The Professor pushed through the crowd and tugged at the arm of a boy he knew from school. "What happened?"

"The van came zooming along just as the lorry started to back out of the lane. I think they didn't notice each other because of the rain and the mud."

The mud? The Professor saw for the first time that the downpour had filled the trench with water and reduced the clay beside it to a treacherous skiddy surface.

"They both tried to stop but the van ran into the trench and the lorry crashed through the garden wall. It sounded like an explosion."

"Was anyone hurt?"

"I don't know but they're all havin' a great fight over it."

And so they were. At the side of the lorry in the wrecked garden, the lorry driver and the foreman in charge of the digging were shouting at the owners of the van, who shouted back equally loudly.

"It was your fault drivin' like that in such dangerous conditions."

"It was the lorry's fault backing out without supervision."

"It wasn't backing out."

"And what about my garden? Will someone tell me that? What about my wall?" cried a small, grey-haired woman.

"What about our livelihood?" the owner of the catering van demanded. "What about our customers?"

The Professor had a sudden image of all those hungry workers with no-one to sell them sandwiches unless, of course, he and Spike...

The Professor pushed further forward, ignoring the protest from the grown-ups, until he had a good view of the van. The whole front of it was smashed and its interior filled with brown water.

They'll never have that back on the road by tomorrow, thought the Professor. It'll take days to dry out.

A squad car came wailing down the road from Irishtown, spraying those whom it passed with mud, and squealed to such a skiddy stop that it almost joined the van in the trench.

A guard got out. "Now then, move back. This is not a variety show."

"Then why did they send you two comedians along to make a bad situation worse, ruining decent people's clothes?" demanded a man as he wiped a splash of mud off his trousers.

The guard ignored the taunt. "Now then, who saw exactly what happened?"

The crowd closed in around the uniformed figures, determined to be heard.

"Hold on a second there..." The foreman began to scramble over the remains of the garden wall. "I said 'Hold on there a second.' Would you mind speaking to those most directly involved in this incident?" He and the caterers helped the householder clamber over the debris of her garden wall. The antagonism between them had vanished as they strove for what they regarded as their proper place at the centre of the enquiry.

But the Professor did not stay to see how things turned out. He had other things to do.

He reached the corner of Strand Road just as Spike came strolling slowly down Beach Road.

"Hey, Spike, guess what? I think I know how to get that seven quid."

Spike's downcast expression vanished. "How?"

"Selling sandwiches. The caterers' van ended up in the trench." The Professor roared laughing. "There I was saying that you could bury a horse in it. But it wasn't a horse that got buried, it was the van."

Spike's depression returned. "We'll never get away with it. We don't know anything about sandwiches."

"What is there to know? You just put bits of ham and things between slices of bread and butter and cut them in half.'

"Where would we get the ham and stuff?"

"Buy it."

"With what?"

"Well with some of my money..." The Professor stood still. "I could get it out of the bank tomorrow. I can ask my mother to come with me."

"Your mother'd want to know what you wanted the money for and she might say 'no'."

"What about Doreen then? Would she lend us the money?"

"She'd want to know what we wanted it for as well. She might want to get in on the act. No. It'll never work unless we keep it secret."

"But it's the best idea that we've had. Maybe we could borrow the things to make the sandwiches."

"But even if we could borrow the things, where would we make the sandwiches and still keep it all a secret?" Then Spike began to stare into the distance; an almost positive sign that he was thinking hard. "My granny is going to be away tomorrow. She's going to visit an old friend of hers down in Kildare on account of it's her eighty-eighth birthday."

"Your Granny is never that old!"

"Not my granny, her friend. Why would my granny go down to Kildare to celebrate her eighty-eighth birthday?"

"Why would her friend?"

"Because she lives down there with her daughter whose husband is a jockey. They are sending a car for her and they'll drive her back. It's my turn to do the shopping for her in the morning."

The Professor nodded and waited.

"She said she'd have to ask the jockey, or whoever brings her back, in for tea. She thought a ham salad would be nice on account of jockeys musn't get fat."

Suddenly the Professor understood. "You mean that we could borrow your granny's stuff to make sandwiches, sell them at a profit, buy more food for your granny with the money we make and have enough left to get the ingredients for more sandwiches the following day?"

"Right." It was Spike's turn to roar with laughter now. "The problem is solved."

For a second, the Professor felt a guilty

twinge. Were they solving their problems at someone else's expense? But then he decided that he was being too sensitive. After all, he hadn't wished for the van to end up in the trench. Such a thought hadn't even entered his mind.

Granny

Chapter Three

ext morning, as early as he could without arousing suspicion, Spike called around to his granny's house.

"Ah, good child. Once I have the shopping in, I can go off with an easy mind. Do you like the new dress?"

Spike thought it looked like all the other blue and pink dresses that his granny had but he said it was very nice.

"Now I want you to go to Morgan's for the ham. They cook their own. Tell them to slice it nice and medium, six slices. Then go to Moore's for the lettuce and tomatoes."

"What about bread?" Spike asked.

"Oh yes, maybe it'd be as well to get a large sliced pan in case the jockey isn't on a diet. In case as well Annie, that's my friend Mrs Hurt, decides to come back with me. I'm going to suggest it as a birthday treat. I've given the place a special clean out."

"It looks lovely," Spike said.

"Well we can only do our best. Oh dear, memories, memories of the good old days. That's what birthdays always bring back to me." For a moment, she seemed all set to have what she called "a bit of a weep." Fortunately, she changed her mind and said, "Don't be too long now. I'm not sure what time they'll be coming for me."

Spike didn't delay for a second on his way to the shops even though the streets offered many distractions such as Eddie Brady with a new bicycle and Martin Loughlin with a hat shaped like an aeroplane.

"I'll see you later, maybe," he said to the two of them.

Morgan's shop was empty and Mrs Morgan didn't seem to be in the mood for chat. "Six slices you said?"

"Yes, please."

"That'll be three pounds fifteen."

Three pounds fifteen! Spike had never considered six slices of ham could be that price.

The lettuce and the tomatoes cost another one pounds fifty. The sliced pan was almost a pound. A grand total of five pounds and sixty-five pence! He'd have to count the number of slices in the pan and get into all kinds of calculations.

Thank heavens for the Professor. He was brilliant at maths.

"You're a topper," Granny said as she examined the purchases. "Everything exactly right. The ham and the vegetables can go into my nice little fridge." She'd had the fridge for as long as Spike could remember but she always referred to it as affectionately as if it were a new kitten. "The bread you can put in the bread bin. I don't care for bread straight out of the fridge."

There was a loud knocking on the front door.

"Merciful hour, that must be the jockey." Granny snatched her handbag from a chair. "And I not nearly ready. Be a pet. Open the door."

Spike had never seen a jockey who wasn't on a horse and, although he had no preconceived ideas, he certainly expected someone much less tall than the man on the doorstep. "Hello," the man said. "I'm Wally Fever come to collect Mrs O'Brien."

"She'll only be a second. She's my granny."

"Going down to visit my granny."

"Oh you're not the jockey?"

"No, that's my father."

"How tall is he then?"

"About this high." Wally held his hand a certain height off the ground.

"And how tall is your mother?"

"About this high." Wally moved his hand to a position half-way between the imagined head of his jockey father and his own head.

Granny O'Brien came fussing down the hall. "Spike, have you no manners? Ask the young man in. It's Wally, isn't it?"

"That's right, Mrs O'Brien."

"You've grown that much since I last saw you."

"I'm nearly nineteen years old now," Wally said by way of explanation.

"Is that right? Nineteen. Honestly, when I think…" For the second time that morning, "a bit of a weep" seemed to be on the way but once more Granny shrugged it off. "Will you come in for a second?"

"We'd be best to make a start before the traffic builds up."

"Well whatever you say yourself. Spike, my case is upstairs."

Spike fetched the small suitcase from the

bedroom.

"Now here's the key of the front door. Lock up before you leave and give the key to your mother. Oh and here's fifty pence for being such a help. No, now take it."

"Well allright." It was after all a kind of a special occasion. And he could use the money towards the cost of the butter for the sandwiches.

"We'll have her back safe and sound tomorrow evening." Wally helped Granny O'Brien into the car.

A question burned in Spike's mind. "How can you be so tall if your father is so small?"

"Just lucky, I guess," Wally said. "Lucky as well that I didn't want to be a jockey."

"What are you going to be then?"

"A pilot. I start training next week."

A pilot! Spike had never thought of being a pilot. In fact since the day that he'd found out about the excursion, he hadn't thought of being anything at all, which was unusual for him. But there was no time to waste over such matters now. He'd go and collect the Professor. The sooner they started on the sandwiches the better. He needn't give Granny's front door key to his mother until she asked him for it. Which she might not do.

Doreen bumped into him at the corner of the street. "What are you up to?" she asked.

"Nothing," said Spike. "I've been shopping for Granny. She's gone to Kildare."

"I know that. I saw her in the car. She waved to me. But you're up to something. I can tell by looking at you."

"Well in that event maybe you can guess what it is by thinking about it."

The Professor was waiting for him at the Martello Tower. "How did it go?"

"Great," Spike said. "She left the key of the house, only I spent five pounds sixty-five on the food. We'll have to be careful what we charge."

"That's means market research," the Professor said. "There are two places in Sandymount Green that sell sandwiches. I asked my mother where she got the sandwich for my lunch yesterday and she said at the Bakery."

From the price list in the Bakery, Spike and the Professor learned that ham sandwiches were 75p and ham and tomatoes 90p. The prices at the Delicatessen across the road were almost the same. The Professor carefully memorised them.

"Keep an eye out for Doreen," Spike said.

"She knows there's something going on."

"Best take the long way round to your granny's house so."

The long way around involved cutting down Newbridge Avenue to the bridge at Lansdowne Road and then along the banks of the Dodder to Londonbridge Road. The remains of the garden wall still blocked the pavement. The digging of the trench seemed to have come to a halt.

"It's probably still full of water. They'll need a pump to empty it out."

"I hope it doesn't rain again at lunchtime," Spike remarked.

"There's not a cloud in the sky," the Professor said, and then remembered how quickly the rain had blown in yesterday. "The main thing is to be at the canal lock when the people come out of the offices."

They hurried across the road, down by the river wall to Ringsend Church and then along by the park to where Granny O'Brien lived. As they went into the house, they heaved great sighs of relief. They were as certain as they could be that they hadn't been seen by Doreen.

"I think we should count the number of slices in the pan first," Spike said, "and see how many sandwiches we can make."

The Professor disagreed. "I think we have to decide how far the ham and stuff will go. After all, there'd be no point in deciding to make up twelve sandwiches if we only had enough filling for eight."

Spike took the ham and salad out of the fridge. "There's six slices of ham. We could cut them in half. That gives us twelve sandwiches, some of them with bits of tomato. We'll charge extra for those like they do in the shops."

"We could make others with just tomato and lettuce. My mother likes that kind of sandwich. There's enough bread to make six of those. That's eighteen altogether. Is there a piece of paper that I could use for calculating?"

Spike opened the drawer in the dresser where Granny O'Brien always kept a pen and old envelopes. The Professor sat down on the table and began to do some sums. "If we are spending five pounds sixty-six pence on ingredients..."

"Make it six pounds on account of the butter," Spike suggested. "It'll be easier to figure out that way."

"O.K. Six pounds is six hundred pence and eighteen sandwiches into six hundred pence is..." The Professor furrowed his brow as he arrived at the answer. "...as close to thirty three pence a sandwich as makes no difference."

"Hey that's great," Spike said. "It's less than half the price in the shops."

"But we have to make a profit of seven pounds and our money back before your Granny gets back from Kildare tomorrow evening," the Professor pointed out. "That's three pounds fifty profit a day. In other words, we should really have divided the sandwiches in nine hundred and fifty pence."

"We'll try and make twenty sandwiches. That way, it'll be easier to decide on the price we have to charge."

"Right." The Professor went back to his calculations. "That is less than forty-eight pence a sandwich even if we charged the same price for all of them, which, of course, we can't do. Those with the ham in them have to cost more."

"Allright," said Spike. "We'll have eight with ham in them, eight with ham and tomatoes and four with lettuce and tomatoes. Forty-eight pence is too difficult. We'd have to keep giving change, whereas if we charged fifty for the tomato and lettuce, fifty-five for the ham and tomato, and sixty for the ham by itself, that'd still give us lots of profit without overcharging." He felt quite dizzy from all the division and addition, unlike the Professor who coolly wrote down the prices of the sandwiches next to his calculation and said, "Let's get started on the sandwiches themselves."

The first problem was that the butter just out of the fridge was too hard to spread. Spike ruined one slice of bread just by trying.

"Maybe if we were to heat it in the oven," suggested the Professor.

Spike put the butter dish in the oven and turned the heat up to medium.

A few minutes later there was a terrible cracking sound. When Spike opened the oven door he found that the butter dish had broken in two and that the butter itself had fallen onto the bottom of the oven where it had instantly melted into a greasy pool. Blue smoke drifted across the kitchen.

"You should always wipe up something like that before it congeals," the Professor advised. "Is there a cloth anywhere?"

"Under the sink."

The Professor tried the door of the cupboard under the sink. It seemed to be stuck. He pulled hard at it. It came right off its hinges.

The Professor went sprawling back against the table.

"Cripes," Spike said. "Now look what you've done."

"It was stuck."

"You're supposed to lift it a bit first."

A packet of detergent fell lazily out of the cupboard, spilling its contents onto the floor.

"Now we'll have to sweep that up," Spike said.

"I didn't do it deliberately," the Professor looked around the kitchen. "Where's the brush?"

"In the scullery. I'll get it." Spike took the fifty pence piece out of his pocket. "You'd better go to the supermarket and buy some margarine while I try to think what to do about the mess in here."

The Professor felt very cross at his stupidity. Even a baby would know not to put a cold glass dish straight out of the fridge into a hot oven. Thank heavens the dish wasn't anything special. There were dozens just like it in the hardware shop. But it meant they'd have to either increase the price of the sandwiches in order to buy a new dish or else cut their profit margins. There was the cupboard door as well. It would all cost money.

He grabbed a package of margarine from the chiller and went to the express checkout.

"Damien?" a voice said questioningly.

It was his mother at the next checkout.

"Oh hello."

"What are you doing here?"

"Spike asked me to buy some margarine."

"My Spike did?"

The Professor swung around in the opposite direction. Mrs O'Halligan was standing in the other checkout queue.

"It's to...to go to his granny's house," the Professor stammered.

"It must be a new fad of hers then," Mrs O'Halligan said, "for I've never known her to eat anything but butter."

"The jockey might be coming to tea."

"The jockey?"

"From Kildare. Spike told me about him."

"Well he knows more than I do so," declared Mrs O'Halligan.

"They have to watch their weight." The Professor wished that the man ahead of him would stop fumbling around in his pocket and find his money quickly.

"Margarine is more a question of fats than weight," the Professor's mother said.

"I'm sure that Spike's granny knows what

she's doing," Mrs O'Halligan said.

"Oh I didn't mean…"

"No, of course, you didn't…"

The man in front of the Professor had finally paid and gone. The Professor handed the fifty pence to the girl, got twopence change and rushed away. "Bye," he said to the two women. "See you later."

Immediately outside the supermarket, he met Doreen.

"What've you got there?"

"Just something." The Professor tried to walk casually away from the supermarket. He managed not to look back until he could do so nice and casually, by making it seem as if he were making sure there was no car turning the corner.

There was no car. Neither, as far as he could tell, was there any Doreen. But just to be on the safe side, he took the long way back to Granny O'Brien's house and felt worn out by the time he was back in the kitchen.

"I met both our mothers and Doreen. But I managed to answer their questions without actually telling a lie. What did you do with the detergent?"

"Put it down the sink," Spike said.

"You managed to fix the cupboard door too."

"No. I just propped it back into place for the moment. But we'd better hurry up and do the sandwiches."

Both Spike and the Professor had often seen sandwiches made. Yet, somehow, when they went about it themselves, it was far from simple. The margarine spread easily enough and a half slice of ham seemed plenty per sandwich. But when they cut the bread in half, they left deep finger marks on it.

They tried washing the finger marks off with hot water but that made the bread limp and soggy.

"The oven's still hot," said Spike. "We could dry them out in there."

"What about the burnt butter? Did you wipe that up?"

"No, I forgot." Spike opened the oven door. A smell of butter came out.

"That smell'll taste the sandwiches," the Professor said, "as well as stink out the house."

"Maybe we'd better open a window." Spike did just that and the smell seemed to lessen. "Could we dry those sandwiches on a tea towel? The one on the hook there looks nice and clean."

The Professor spread the tea towel on the

kitchen table. Spike carefully placed the two damp sandwiches on one half and folded the other half over it.

They were much more careful with the next six sandwiches, which didn't look too bad. However, the eight ham and tomato sandwiches were much more difficult. Every time they tried to cut them in half without squashing them, the pieces of tomato slid out onto the table. Some of the pieces even fell onto the floor.

The Professor said, "We can't use those."

"We could wash them first."

"That'd only make the sandwiches all wet again. I think maybe we should slice the bread in half before we put the ham and the tomato on it."

Painstakingly, so as not to damage the bread, they removed the ham and tomato and cut the slices of bread in half. But they'd forgotten that some of the margarine had stuck to the filling and so there was the problem of lifting the ham and tomato off the kitchen table.

By the time they'd managed it, the ham and tomato were definitely looking badly battered. "But still," Spike said, "that won't be noticed inside a sandwich."

And in a way he was right. A customer might not guess that what he was eating had been stuck to a table.

Having learned from the first sixteen sandwiches, the last four didn't present so many problems although the Professor thought maybe they should have cut up the lettuce instead of just putting it in in leaves. But Spike said they were running out of time and that hungry people wouldn't be that fussy.

Then a thought occurred to them, something they ought to have considered from the very beginning. How were they going to get twenty sandwiches from Granny O'Brien's to Baggot Street Bridge?

"We'll need a box of some kind," the Professor said.

"There's a hat box upstairs on top of the wardrobe," Spike said.

Spike ran up to the bedroom and lifted down the box off the wardrobe. There were two hats inside; one made of straw and the other of a pale green velvety material. Spike had never seen his granny wear either of them, which must mean that they were very old. It couldn't matter if they were left on the bed for a few hours.

The Professor looked doubtfully at the box. "It's very big. The sandwiches would look lost in it."

"Maybe we could pad it out with newspapers." Spike took some newspapers from the bucket at the back door. There were bits of coal and turf on them but time was now really running out, so the Professor and Spike just folded and twisted the papers until the box was half-filled.

"That's a bit better if it wasn't so springy. Maybe if we put a dish or a big plate on top of the paper and the sandwiches on the dish, they wouldn't bounce around," the Professor said.

Spike took the large dish that Granny O'Brien served the Christmas turkey off from under the wash stand in the hall. It was slightly larger than the box but, with a bit of wriggling and pushing and stretching, the boys finally managed to fit it on top of the newspapers.

They carefully arranged the sandwiches, including the two from the tea towel, on the dish. Then they covered the box with the tea towel to keep the dust off the food. Then they tried to lift the box. It was very heavy. "We need something to transport it," said the

Professor.

"There's an old pram outside," Spike said. "But would that not attract too much attention?"

"Not at all," replied the Professor. "I've often seen people pushing old prams in Dublin. And at least it'd be quick."

The pram proved to be older than Spike remembered and very rickety. But the Professor said that beggars couldn't be choosers so they put the box of sandwiches into the pram and pushed it out into the back lane.

The few people they passed on their way to Bath Avenue didn't give them a second glance. Spike began to feel that the Professor had been right when he had said no-one would pay any attention to the pram. Maybe people would have continued to ignore them if it hadn't been for the trench on Londonbridge Road.

The digging work here had closed one pavement to pedestrians and the pavement on the other side of the road had cars parked on it so there was not enough room for the pram. Spike and the Professor finally had to push it along the road. And the road was particularly busy with traffic, which deeply resented having to slow down behind the two boys.

Worse was to follow. A hunk of the garden wall was still lying close to where the boys had to pass and, much as they tried to avoid it, the pram seemed to suddenly develop a will of its own and head straight for it.

"Pull as hard as you can," Spike yelled.

"I am," the Professor yelled back, "but it's like one of those trolleys in the supermarket that won't go where you want it. Maybe if we were to deliberately head for a bit of wall, the pram'd go in the opposite direction."

The boys tried this manoeuvre but it only resulted in them reaching the chunk of wall all the more quickly and hitting it with such force that the hatbox bounced up in the air.

"Well, aren't you the right pair of eejits!" a man with a newspaper said.

"Maybe it's some kind of new game," a woman with a walking stick suggested.

More grown-ups gathered as Spike and the Professor struggled to get the pram going in the right direction.

Martin Loughlin, his airplane hat on the back of his head, appeared as if from nowhere. "What are you at?" he asked.

"Nothing," said Spike. "It's a kind of message."

He knew that Martin Loughlin hated going for messages and to even mention the word would get rid of him. But the grown-ups seemed to have nothing better to do than stand and watch.

"They'll attract the guards if we aren't careful," the Professor said.

"Once we get across the main road we'll be fine," Spike said.

But they weren't fine at all. The pram had a kind of seizure in the middle of the pedestrian crossing and its wheels ceased to turn.

A lorry driver yelled, "Are you colour blind or what? Can you not see the light is changed? Move that contraption or I'll squash it!"

Between them, Spike and the Professor just about managed to lift the pram onto the next pavement. They looked up Haddington Road and, for the first time, realised how steeply it rose before reaching Baggot Street Bridge.

"We'll never make it by lunchtime," Spike said.

"We have to make it," replied the Professor. "It's too late to turn back now. We'll leave the pram in here to the side and carry the box. If we take turns we can manage."

The box seemed to be even heavier than when they had lifted it into the pram. Spike volunteered to carry it first but, after about ten yards, he began to sweat so much that he couldn't see where he was going.

"Maybe if we were to take the dish out of the box," the Professor said.

"But it's my granny's hatbox."

"We can hide it in a front garden. There's one here that looks as though nobody ever goes near it."

Carefully, the Professor lifted the dish of sandwiches out of the hatbox. Spike took the box and hid it under a bush in the overgrown garden.

"I can manage," the Professor said. "It's much easier without the hatbox."

"Maybe we should have done it this way from the the start," said Spike.

"No, no. We'd never have got this far without dropping it all."

Spike saw the sense to this and the pram and the box would easily be got back to his granny's house once there were no sandwiches to worry about. Baggot Street Bridge came into sight. The first of the office workers were already gathering around the canal lock.

"I'll bet they'll be starving and wondering where the mobile caterers are." The Professor grinned. "Won't they get a surprise when they see us?"

And indeed the workers did get a surprise when they saw Spike and the Professor, sweaty and dusty, appearing on the banks of the Grand Canal with a large dish covered with a cloth through which large spots of grease were appearing.

But the Professor and Spike were so relieved to have arrived there safely that they were quite unaware of the effect that they were having on their prospective customers.

"Sandwiches, sandwiches, lovely sandwiches," Spike declared in the way he'd heard stall-holders in the city streets advertise their wares. "Ham, ham and tomato, lettuce and tomato. Freshly cut, freshly made. Professor, let the people see the goods."

The Professor was so carried away by the brilliance of Spike's sales promotion that, with a magician-like movement, he swept the tea-towel off the sandwiches and presented them for approval.

Rarely had so unappetising a sight been seen at that particular canal lock or, indeed, at any canal lock in the whole of Ireland. The bump that the pram had got in Londonbridge Road had seriously disarranged the sandwiches. Having to carry the pram had caused further damage as, no doubt, the removing of them from the box had.

Also, in some mysterious way, particles of coal from the newspaper had settled on the food and now glistered darkly in the little pools of melted margarine that had formed on the last stage of the journey up Haddington Road.

Both boys stared in dismay at the confusion of bread and coal, ham and tomatoes, lettuce and margarine.

The Professor made a desperate attempt to rearrange the display into something more appealing. He only managed to create something slightly more appalling, for his hands had somehow become absolutely filthy since leaving the house.

"Are you seriously offering those for sale?" a blonde woman with bright red lips demanded.

"Of course we are," Spike said crossly. "The usual van had an accident. We thought you'd be hungry."

"It's not hungry but mad we'd have to be to eat something like that."

"What'll you eat then?"

"There's lots of shops around here that sell sandwiches. We only buy from the van because it's convenient. Anyway, do you not need a licence to sell stuff in public?"

"There's the Department of Health regulations too," chipped in a fellow in a bright green suit and a moustache that looked like the tail of a dead cat. "You're probably breaking all kinds of laws."

"But what are we going to do with the sandwiches?" asked the Professor.

"Clear off out of here with them. That's what you're going to do." It was the driver of the mobile van with a big tray hung around his neck on which were the most perfect looking sandwiches all wrapped in cellophane. Beside him was his wife, pushing a trolley with tins of drink and fresh fruit. She had a big piece of sticking plaster across her forehead.

"Such cheek," she said, "trying to take advantage."

"We didn't know you'd be able to get here today," the Professor said.

"Well we did manage it. Now clear off before I call the police. In fact I might call them anyway, trying to sell things like this to the public. Did you never hear of food poisoning?" the van man demanded.

The van woman said, "Maybe we should get that guard we saw just now in case they've managed to persuade anyone to buy any of this muck already."

"It's not muck," Spike said. "It's the best that money can buy. We have to sell them or we'll be in terrible trouble."

"You'll be in worse trouble if you stay here," the van man said. Then, turning to the workers, he asked, "Now then folks, who wants what today?"

As the van owners were surrounded by customers the Professor said to Spike, "It's no good. We'd best get out of here before the guard sees us." He covered the sandwiches with the cloth. "We'll just have to think of something else."

"Like what?" Spike asked.

"Maybe the fellows who dig the trench wouldn't be so particular."

Spike and the Professor studied each other's expressions to make sure they weren't just trying to cheer each other up.

They were delighted to see that they weren't.

"We should have thought of that in the first place," Spike said. "It would have saved us the long walk up here."

"Yeh, but we'll know better tomorrow. We just have to find somewhere quiet now to make this lot look better."

The Professor led the way back down Haddington Road. He thought for a second of going into the church to fix the sandwiches and then decided that somehow this would not be right. Instead he said to Spike, "We'll do it in the garden where we left the hatbox."

Chapter Four

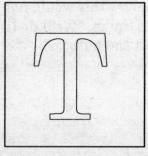he two boys hauled the hatbox out from under the hedge.

"Cripes, what a terrible smell," Spike said. "It's worse than the melted butter."

"You often get that in a neglected garden," the Professor said. "Rotting vegetation."

"I hope it's nothing dead, like a cat."

"Of course it isn't. We'd see a dead cat and not just smell it. How clean are your hands?"

"Not very."

"We can wipe them on the newspapers in the hatbox," said the Professor.

They did this and ended up with great streaks of black from the coaldust.

"That's worse," Spike said.

"We'd better get rid of the newspapers or more of it'll get on the bread." The Professor rolled up the newspaper into a tight ball and placed it momentarily under the hedge.

"What the blazes is going on out there?" It was another adult, this time a purple-faced man with carrot-coloured hair leaning out of a top floor window of the house. "What are you two up to down there?"

"Nothing," Spike said, rising to his feet while the Professor tried to do a quick tidying job on the sandwiches.

"Nothing, how are you! Do you think I haven't been watching you for the last few minutes, destroying my garden, putting rubbish under the hedge?"

"We thought the house was empty," Spike explained, "and we were going to take the newspapers with us."

"Oh were you indeed? And what have you got on that big dish? Stolen, no doubt."

The Professor stood up indignantly. "We most certainly did not steal anything. We are involved in a straightforward commercial transaction."

"Oh yes, so straightforward that it involves trespass and skulking around."

"We're sorry if…"

Spike tugged at the Professor's arm. "Come on," he said. "It's no good arguing with him. He's like the people at the bridge. Once they get an idea in their minds, you can't shift it. It's my turn to carry the sandwiches. You take the box."

"But he thinks we're thieves..."

"That's right," the houseowner yelled. "That's exactly what I do think. And I'm coming down to see for myself exactly what it is you have there." As abruptly as it had appeared, the man's head disappeared.

"Will you come on, Professor? Things are bad enough without making them worse." Spike ran out of the front garden.

The Professor hesitated for a moment, still reluctant to leave without convincing the man of their innocence. Then he had to admit that Spike was right. There were times when it was best to retreat. The Professor grabbed the newspaper from under the hedge, popped it in the box and followed his friend back to where the pram was still parked.

"Where's the dishcloth?" the Professor asked.

"The dishcloth?" Spike looked back up the road. "We must have dropped it. We'd better go back and look for it."

The red-haired man was standing in the middle of the road, trying see where the boys had gone.

"We'll never get past him," said the Professor. "And the men on the road works will have had their lunch if we delay anymore. First things first. And the first thing we have to do is to sell these sandwiches. How do you think they look?"

"Not too bad," Spike said hopefully. "If you were really hungry that is. But there's that funny smell."

"It seems to be coming off the box." The Professor sniffed at the box. "Good thing it's made of strong cardboard. It'll stand up to being cleaned but we'd better not put it too near the food."

"So what goes in the pram? The food or the box?" asked Spike.

"I think the food should. It'll keep the sun off it…"

"Maybe we should see if the pram will go properly before we put anything into it. Can you manage the sandwiches as well as the box?"

"Well, for a few seconds." The Professor carefully adjusted his balance as Spike placed the dish of sandwiches on top of the cardboard box.

Spike gave the pram a slight push. The wheels seemed to turn correctly. He took the dish back from the Professor and placed it in the pram. The two boys began to walk slowly towards Londonbridge Road. This time the pram did not stall in the middle of the crossing.

Things were once more beginning to look hopeful.

"What's that you have there?"

It was yet another grown-up, this time a friend of Granny O'Brien.

"Just a few things," Spike said.

"A few things…" The woman peered short-sightedly into the pram. "It looks to me for all the world like…"

But Spike did not stop to hear the end of the remark.

The Professor smiled sweetly. "Nothing at all to worry about, Ma'am." He'd heard the plumber speak like that to his mother when the upstairs tank burst and flooded the house.

"Worry?" Then the woman's expression changed. "What's that terrible smell?"

"Keep walking," Spike said under his breath. "Just keep walking. She'll get fed up following us, like all the others did."

"I never realised until now how fond of interfering grown-ups that we don't even know could be," the Professor muttered back.

"It's because they've too much spare time," Spike explained, "especially when they're off work. They need something to occupy themselves with. But she could be worse than the others. She knows my granny."

"Then we'd better walk faster."

"I'm pushing the pram as hard as I can now."

"I'll just have to push it along with you then."

The Professor managed to tuck the hatbox under one arm without squashing it too much and, with his free arm, he gripped the handle of the pram. Together the two boys pushed as hard as they could.

The pram, however didn't respond very well to this treatment and once more began to behave as though it had a will all its own, choosing the direction it preferred to go. And that direction was towards the middle of the road.

"We'll be killed," the Professor gasped.

"We'll have to stop and carry it again. It's only a few more yards to the hut. I can hear the men talking."

"It means putting the box in the pram."

"That won't matter for a few seconds, I hope." Spike glanced over his shoulder.

His granny's friend had been slowed down by the roadworks, ending up on the stretch of pavement between the trench and the broken garden walls. She was slowly picking her way over a small pile of clay, still slippery from yesterday's rainstorm.

Spike said, "We might get our business settled before she catches up with us. She's afraid of falling into the trench."

"I don't blame her for that." The Professor could see that large sections of the trench were filled with thick brown muck. "They haven't managed to clean it out yet."

"Yes, well talking of clearing things out, we'd best put the pram down and let you lift out the box. The smell from it is getting stronger."

The two boys put the pram down on the road.

The Professor lifted out the hatbox.

"Maybe you should wait here for me with the pram and the hatbox. I'll manage the sandwiches by myself," Spike said.

Spike gingerly lifted the dish of sandwiches. The Professor moved to help him. Somehow between them they slipped. Spike, who was standing on the edge of the trench, fell backwards with the dish and vanished with a shriek of terror down into the mud.

The pram, as though terrified by the noise, rolled on down the road until it hit the side of the workmen's hut and disintegrated into several large pieces.

For a terrible moment, the world seemed to stand still. Then the Professor flung himself to the edge of the trench.

Spike, now bright brown in colour, was slipping and sliding around as he tried to get a foothold. The dish had sunk without trace, leaving the sandwiches to form a very strange pattern on top of the mud.

"Your hand," the Professor said. "Give me your hand."

Spike wiped his eyes and, with the Professor's help, pulled himself up out of the trench.

The two boys stared at each other, horrified.

The workmen, having recovered from the attack on their hut by the pram, came rushing towards the two boys. There expressions were a mixture of concern and indignation.

"Have yez got no more sense than to go falling into the trench?" the foreman demanded. "Do you not realise that yez could be seriously injured?"

"And who flung that pram at the hut?"

demanded the lorry driver. "That's what I want to know."

"The pram is theirs," declared Granny's friend, who had finally caught up with them.

"It was an accident," the Professor said. "It was all a terrible accident. I'm sorry. We'll come back for the pram later." He grabbed Spike by the arm and propelled him towards the Dodder, picking up the hatbox from beside the hut.

"But there's the dish as well, there's my Granny's dish," Spike spluttered as he brushed the mud from his mouth.

"The first thing is to get you looking less like a mudman and more like a human," declared the Professor.

"My mother'll kill me," Spike said.

"She won't be even able to recognise you if that mud hardens on you."

"What are we going to do?"

"Take you home to my place. Mum is reading a book out on the patio. We can get in through the garage. While you have a shower, I'll put your things in the washing machine."

"Are you sure you know how to work the washing machine? I don't want my clothes ruined as well as everything else."

"The machine is fully automatic. I've often

used it before. And even if your clothes were ruined, how much worse off would that make us than we are right now?" The Professor tightened his grip on the hatbox. At least they hadn't lost that.

Chapter Five

rs O'Neill remained totally unaware that her son and Spike had crept into the house. The two boys could see her outline against the patio door as she sat on her chair.

"Take your shoes off here," the Professor said, "otherwise there'll be mud all over the place."

It was on the tip of Spike's tongue to ask if Mrs O'Neill would even notice such a thing. But then he decided that such flippancy wouldn't help, so he did as he was told while the Professor fetched a black rubbish sack.

"Put your clothes in here when you've undressed. The bathroom is at the top of the stairs. I'll keep an eye on Mum in case she comes indoors and starts asking questions."

As the boys busied themselves with their

tasks, Spike, with getting rid of the mud, the Professor with watching Spike's clothes revolve in the washing machine, they couldn't help feeling worried.

The morning had been a total disaster. Far from solving anything, their excursion into the sandwich business had put them in a hopeless situation. There was the lost dish, the lost dishcloth, the smashed pram, the cupboard door, the cost of replacing Granny O'Brien's food, the butter dish, the terrible smell of the hatbox, which was now out in the garage.

The Professor realised that the box might be safe enough there for a while but, even if his mother didn't notice the smell, his father would become aware of it as soon as he drove his car in.

There was really only one thing to be done.

Spike, under the shower, was coming to the same conclusion and he would not delay about saying it straight out to the Professor.

There was a knock on the bathroom door. "Hey, I've got your clothes. They're a bit hot from the dryer."

"That's allright."

The Professor opened the bathroom door and put Spike's clothes on a chair. "I've been thinking."

"So have I," said Spike.

"Oh?"

"Yey. I've decided that I can't go on the excursion to Cork even if I had the money."

"I've decided the same thing," the Professor sighed.

"But you have the money..."

"I know, but the sandwich idea was really mine..."

"No, it wasn't," protested Spike.

"Yes, it was. I thought of it when I saw the van in the trench."

"You saw me in the trench as well but that doesn't mean you were to blame for me being in it."

"Well maybe we're both to blame. But the thing we have to do now is to put things right for your granny. We can use my money for that."

"Won't your parents want to know what you've spent the money on if you don't go on the excursion?"

"I'll just say I needed it for something else," the Professor said. "They trust me. Bring the towel down with you when you've dried yourself. I'll put it in the laundry basket. Oh, and give the shower basin a good wipe."

"O.K." Spike pulled the plug and the basin began to empty with a great gurgling noise.

Mrs O'Neill, pausing at the end of a chapter, heard the noise and thought, "We'll have to get that plumber back while the fine weather is here. I don't like that sound at all." Then she wondered who could be in the bathroom. She placed her book on the ground beside her and went into the house. "Damien? Is that you?"

"Yes, Mum."

"I didn't hear you come in."

"We didn't want to disturb you."

"Who is 'we'?"

"Spike. He's having a wash. He fell."

"As long as he hasn't hurt himself."

"No, he's grand."

"Is there something wrong?"

"Not really."

"That's not much of an answer."

Fortunately, at the moment, Spike came downstairs. Mrs O'Neill had never seen him look so rosy and clean. "Maybe you should fall down more often," she said, "only don't tell your mother I said that."

"I wasn't going to mention it to my mother at all," Spike replied with complete truthfulness.

"You could start a new fashion with that

hairstyle."

Spike caught a glimpse of himself in a looking glass. A piece of hair, just like the one that had earned him his nickname, was standing up off the back of his head. He patted it but it refused to lie down.

"You need a comb," Mrs O'Neill said.

"There's one upstairs," the Professor said.

"There's one here as well." Mrs O'Neill opened a drawer and took out a comb. She watched Spike struggle to comb his hair flat. When at last he'd managed it, she said, "Are the two of you sure there's nothing wrong?"

"No, no, nothing." Both boys spoke at once.

"What was all that about margarine this morning? Spike's mother says that his granny never uses it."

"We thought it'd make a ...a kind of..." Spike struggled for the right words.

"Surprise? Well maybe you should have waited and asked her first. Not everyone likes that kind of surprise. Still now I must get back to my book. The newspaper wants my review by tomorrow. And look at the time! Spike, do you want to stay and eat with us? It won't be much, just another sandwich, I'm afraid."

Another sandwich? What did Mrs O'Neill mean by the word 'another'? Did she know more than she was letting on?

The Professor, realising what was going through Spike's mind, quickly said, "Mum means that we had sandwiches for lunch yesterday as well."

"Does Spike not like sandwiches? Do you not, Spike?"

"Oh it's not that at all... It's just that they'll be expecting me home."

"Well if you're sure..."

"Yes, thanks, Mrs O'Neill." He glanced at the Professor. "I'll see you later at the Tower."

"O.K. At two o'clock."

The Professor let Spike out by the front door. Spike whispered, "Don't forget the hatbox."

"Don't worry."

The Professor went into the kitchen. His mother was buttering bread. "Well at least they'll be home-made sandwiches today. Ham and tomato. I bought it all fresh in the supermarket this morning."

Ham and tomato! The Professor had a sudden image of pieces of bread and meat floating on top of thick brown mud. But he daren't rouse any suspicions. "That'll be fine, Mum," he said gallantly.

"Good," Mrs O'Neill said.

In Spike's house, fresh fish was being served for the mid-day meal; coated in breadcrumbs just the way Spike liked it but, like the Professor, he was finding difficulty in eating.

"What's the matter?" asked his mother.

"Nothing," Spike said.

"Maybe you're doing too much running around in the sun," suggested his father. "According to the news, this is one of the warmest days on record."

Mention of the heat of the day reminded Spike of the way the sandwiches had melted under the cloth. For a second, he thought he might actually be sick but he forced himself to eat the fish.

"You swallowed that as though it was medicine." His mother carefully examined his face. Are your sure you feel all right?"

"Yes, I'm grand," Spike said and then had to resist an almost overwhelming urge to add, "apart from the fact that myself and the Professsor stole Granny's food, lost her dishcloth and dish, wrecked her pram, broke her butter dish and the door of her cupboard and now don't dare walk up either Londonbridge Road or Haddington Road in case we get chased by a group of workmen, two sandwich sellers and a bad-tempered householder." Oh yes, indeed, Spike felt grand; like a condemned man waiting for sentence to be carried out.

And how much longer could he and the Professor get away with it? As it was, he'd only had time to throw his granny's hatbox into her yard before Doreen had come rushing around the corner.

She'd looked at him in much the same way as his mother was looking at him now but the most important difference was that Doreen, as ever, suspected he was up to something. She had actually said as much to him.

She had said, "You look all different."

Spike had tried to dodge the issue by saying, "We'll be late for dinner."

But now Doreen was looking at him again in the same interested way.

And as soon as their mother went to get the dessert, Doreen said, "I know what it is. You look all clean; not just your face but everything, your clothes, everything."

"What was that you said?" Mrs O'Halligan called from the kitchen.

"Oh nothing, Mammy. Will I clear the places?"

"Yes, do. There's a good girl."

Doreen couldn't resist a smirk as she took Spike's plate from in front of him, and whispered, "Whatever it is, you won't get away with it for long."

Mrs O'Halligan confirmed Doreen's prophecy when she brought in dishes of ice-cream and bananas. "I met that friend of yours, the Professor, in the supermarket. He said he was buying margarine for your granny."

"Margarine is supposed to be good for you," Spike answered, hoping that that didn't count as a lie.

"Lovely bananas." His father smacked his lips.

Mrs O'Halligan responded at once to his words of praise. "I knew you'd like them although it's a disgrace what they charge for them. When I think what we used to get them for in Moore Street."

"We had this, or something very like it, the first time we went out together."

Mrs O'Halligan smiled. "Oh indeed, a banana split in Cafolla's of O'Connell Street."

Spike sighed an inward sigh of relief. Once his parents started talking about old times, they could get very soft-eyed and romantic, a bit like his granny with her "weeps."

"And the crowds on the buses coming out to the strand on Sundays. But now you're lucky if you can get a bus."

"Did I tell you what I heard a women say in the bus queue outside Clery's?" Mr O'Halligan asked. "We'd been waiting the best part of an hour. And suddenly she said, 'Do you know why this service is called the banana run?' 'No,' I said, 'why?' 'Because,' she said , "the buses come in bunches'."

Spike thought that was the silliest joke he had ever heard but Mrs O'Halligan and Doreen almost split their sides laughing.

"Oh dear, oh dear," Mrs O'Halligan said, "as long as there is a laugh to be had, we'll never die crying, oh but if only...'

"I know, I know," Mr O'Halligan reached out and touched his wife's hand, "but maybe things'll get better now with the warm weather. Places often take on extra people during the summer."

Mrs O'Halligan said, "It's not your fault. And I know that I take it out on you and on the children as well sometimes."

Spike gave her a hug. So did Doreen.

"You're good children," Mrs O'Halligan said.

Spike felt himself thoroughly ashamed and was aware once more of Doreen studying him carefully.

Mrs O'Halligan released them and said, "Well, and what have the two of you on for this afternoon?"

"Oh nothing much, just messing around with the Professor."

"I thought I might go to the dogshow in Sandymount Green," Doreen still had her eyes fixed on Spike. "There's a ten-pound prize for the best dog."

"Maybe I should borrow a dog and enter," Mrs O'Halligan said jokingly, but Doreen took the remark seriously.

"Oh no," she said. "It's only for the under-fourteens. It's to mark the start of Young Persons' Activities Week. There are posters all over the place."

Spike remembered vaguely seeing some of these posters but he and the Professor hadn't stopped to look at them. Now Doreen was teasing him with talk about a ten-pound prize. But worse was to come.

"Mrs Nolan says I can borrow her dog, Terry, and enter him. He's a lovely dog, so nice and friendly. Is it all right if I go and collect him now?"

"Yes, of course, it is, only be careful crossing the roads."

"Is it all right if I go as well?" Spike asked.

"Yes of course, and remember what you father said about not doing too much running around in the sun." Mrs O'Halligan smiled at her husband as Spike banged the front door. "I think it might do us a bit of good if we were to get out of the house for a while as well, just a stroll along Strand Road."

"You're dead right," Mr O'Halligan said, "it might be raining tomorrow. Come on and I'll give you a hand with the wash-up."

Mrs O'Halligan laughed, "Well, no doubt but wonders will never cease. You'll be getting the tea ready next!"

Brandy

Chapter Six

pike caught up with Doreen at the next corner. "What time does this dog show start?"

"That's for me to know and for you to find out."

"You're being rotten."

"And so are you. You won't even tell me what you and the Professor wanted the margarine for."

"It has to do with the excursion to Cork and Kinsale."

Doreen moved on angrily. "Well, of course, if you're going to make stupid remarks..."

"It wasn't a stupid remark. Honestly, Doreen, it wasn't. But there are more important things now than the excursion."

"Such as what?"

"I can't tell you. Not that I don't trust you. I

just can't tell you. But the Professor and I have to win that dog show."

"How can you do that if you don't have a dog? And no, you can't take Terry. Mrs Nolan said she would only trust me to take him on the lead to Sandymount Green. And, if Terry wins, Mrs Nolan and I are going to divide the money. That was our agreement."

"Well at least tell me what time it's at and what we have to do to enter."

Doreen relented. "All right, I'll tell you but I don't see what good it'll do you. The show begins at two fifteen. You can get an entry form in the hall next to the Methodist Church; the one with the nice tree in front."

"Thanks."

"Oh that's all right but I still don't know where you'll get a dog. They'll all be gone by now."

And, indeed, as she walked along Strand Road, Spike could see the truth of Doreen's words for down every side road he looked there seemed to be children of all ages and sizes with dogs of all ages and sizes.

The Professor was on his usual seat by the Tower, staring glumly out to sea. Without waiting for Spike to sit, he began to talk. "We've made a right mess of things. I wish we'd never heard of the excursion. I'll never be able to eat properly again."

"I was thinking the very same thing. Then I found out from Doreen about the dog show in the Green."

"Oh that," said the Professor.

"You mean you knew about it?"

"Yes, but we haven't got a dog."

"We could have borrowed one only now it's too late," Spike said crossly.

"You mean you don't have to own the dog? You can use someone else's dog?"

"Doreen is entering Mrs Nolan's Terry. And I saw a whole lot of kids just now with dogs that don't belong to them."

The Professor was suddenly looking brighter. "I know a dog we might be able to use. It belongs to Miss Finucane, who lives in one of those mews houses near Merrion Gates. I heard her telling my mother the other day that she never has the time to exercise the poor brute properly, so in a way we'd be doing her a favour."

"It might be as well if we didn't mention the dog show. Doreen has to split any money she wins with Mrs Nolan."

"Well actually," the Professor said, "Miss Finucane might not be home. She works in town in the Department of Enlightenment. We'd have to get the dog in and out of her garden by ourselves."

Spike felt a sudden twinge of doubt. "Breaking and entering, they call that."

"The same could be said of us using your granny's place this morning."

"No, they couldn't. We had a key."

"All right then. We'll talk to my mother."

Mrs O'Neill was surprised to see the two boys back so soon. She'd finished reading the book and was about to start writing her review. She hoped Spike and the Professor weren't going to play in the garden. That would ruin her concentration. She was quite relieved when her son said, "Spike and I thought we might take Miss Finucane's dog out."

"Oh yes, I'm sure she'd love that. So would the dog!"

"Good," said her son and, as unexpectedly as they had arrived, the boys departed.

The mews houses were only a few minutes run away. The back gardens were enclosed by high brick walls. The gate into Miss Finucane's was locked but Spike and the Professor quickly climbed over it. A dog, quite big and dark brown in colour, backed into a corner and bared its teeth. Fortunately, the Professor remembered its name, "Here, Brandy. Here, Brandy. Good dog."

The dog, far from becoming more friendly, regarded with increased suspicion this strange boy who knew his name.

"You'll get nowhere like that with him," declared Spike. "You have to get him excited, take his mind off things. Like this." Spike ran quickly around the garden and shouted, "The cat! The cat! Where's the cat?"

The dog's jaw dropped open in amazement.

"Do you see what I mean?" said Joe. "He's getting interested."

Certainly it seemed to the Professor that Brandy was less hostile. Maybe Spike had the right approach. The Professor did a circuit of the garden too. "The cat! Where's the cat?"

Spike ran in the opposite direction and yelled. "The cat! The bird! The horse! Where'd they go? For a walk? Did they go for a walk?"

It was the word 'walk' that really did the trick for suddenly Brandy joined the two boys in their runabout, snapping and keening at their heels.

"Whoa, boy," Spike said, slowing down. But Brandy, once started, didn't want to stop. These two boys, who only a few seconds ago had seemed like a major threat to his security, had now become the bringers of freedom and release from the boredom of waiting for his owner to return. A walk? He simply had to show his gratitude! He simply had to leap and lick and shove and to continue doing all of these things even when the dark-haired one who had spoken the magic word 'walk' fell over onto the ground.

"Would you get him off," Spike yelled, "or I'll be as dirty as when I fell into the trench."

The Professor grabbed Brandy's collar and hauled him away from Spike. "Good boy," he said, "good boy."

But Brandy continued to wriggle and keen and slobber, and his eyes were turning around in his head.

"I think we went too far," the Professor panted. "I think we over-excited him."

"He'll calm down when we get him on the road," Spike dusted himself off. "The thing is how do we do that. There's no key in the gate."

"Could we try lifting him? Or would that make him even worse than he is?"

"We need something to control him with, a lead of some kind."

The two boys looked around the garden. Rolled up near a small shed was an old clothes line.

"That'll do great." Spike fetched the line while the Professor held on to Brandy.

Spike slipped the rope through the dog's collar and tied a knot. "O.K. Now it'll be easier if we get him on top of the shed."

Brandy began to back away as though he understood what Spike had said.

Spike decided to rouse his interest again. "Good dog, nice dog. Big walk, big jump."

The word "walk" once more had the desired effect. Brandy almost knocked the Professor off his feet as he jumped up on top of the shed beside Spike and once more began to lavish tokens of gratitude on him.

Spike kept the dog at arm's length as the Professor climbed up next to them.

"What I suggest is this," said Spike. "I sit on the wall and you hand Brandy over to me. Then you sit on the wall. Then I jump down off the wall and you hand Brandy down to me."

Well, of course, that plan had no hope of working and didn't. Spike climbed on top of the wall easily enough. But when the Professor tried to hand Brandy over, the dog panicked and knocked Spike down into the lane. Then after a moment's hesitation the dog jumped down and landed safely on Spike. He at once recommenced washing Spike's face.

"Grab the rope in case he panics," the Professor yelled.

Spike was just in time, for Brandy suddenly remembered the purpose of all this activity, as he understood it, was a walk on the Strand. He was about to achieve this ambition when Spike, winded as he was, managed to catch the end of the rope. He held on until the Professor landed beside him and relieved him of the task.

The Professor looked at his watch. "It's five past two," he said, "we'll have to hurry."

Hurrying suited Brandy. He loved running along with the two boys even though they weren't headed for the strand. Maybe it was part of the fun. Maybe they'd get to the strand eventually. Brandy had very little experience of human beings, apart from Miss Finucane. And Miss Finucane never ran. She strolled. Very slowly.

It was ten past two when the boys and Brandy got to the hall and asked for the entry form. The woman in charge said, "You're only just in time. Is that dog all right?"

Brandy's tongue was lolling out of the side of his mouth. There was definitely something almost crazed about the expression in his eyes.

"He's grand," Spike said.

"Which category? Special breed or household pet?"

Remembering Brandy's expressions of affection, the boys said at the same time, "Household pet."

"All right. Here's your number. Stick one on the dog's collar. Keep the other one safe. You might need it later."

Brandy tried to eat the number that was to go on his collar but Spike somehow prevented him from doing this.

"Hurry along. The judging begins in a few minutes."

"What did you put on the entry form?" Spike asked as they left the hall.

"I put your name and my address," the Professor replied. "That seemed the best solution if we win."

"WHEN we win," Spike corrected. Then he and the Professor stopped and stared in amazement at the scene inside Sandymount Green. They'd never seen so many dogs in one place.

And yet everything was strangely calm as though dogs and humans were awed by the seriousness of the occasion, by the knowledge that one of them would be selected by the two women on the platform in the centre of the Green as the best entrant in his class.

The largest of the women, dressed in very heavy tweeds for so warm a day, was already silently selecting and rejecting the animals on the grass.

Her companion, dressed as if for a wedding in a pale green dress and a matching hat that had several bits and pieces hanging from it, stared up at the sky as though asking the Almighty why He had allowed her to become involved in such an event.

The largest of the women stopped staring at the animals and looked at her watch, counting the few minutes that remained before judging would officially begin.

"Quick," Spike said, "We'd better get in whichever is our section."

"I don't think we've been divided into sections yet," the Professor replied, and had no sooner finished speaking than the woman in tweeds, as if by magic, held up a small hailer. She spoke into it with an abruptness that caused a wave of unease among the waiting animals. "Pets to the left. Best of class to the right."

Then, seeing the confusion that this

instruction caused, she said with increased loudness. "This is my left hand. All those who have entered in the pet section, move over to this side of the Green."

"Come on. We'd better join in or she might eliminate us." The Professor dragged at the clothes line but Brandy was suddenly like a statue, refusing to move.

"And special breed, or class, as I believe professionals like to call it," she glared coldly at her colleague who continued to stare at the sky, "over to this side of the Green."

There was more confusion, but nothing such as was yet to come, as dogs were moved to the appropriate side of the Green. One or two animals even gave a slight whine which the tweedy woman stopped with a glare.

The Professor pulled on the clothes line again. And again Brandy failed to move.

The tweedy woman noticed them. "If you are intending to enter that dog, you should be inside the railings, not outside on the path."

"Brandy, will you move?" the Professor asked.

Doreen was staring open-mouthed with Terry lying at her feet.

"Will I give him a bit of a prod?" Spike asked. But before the Professor could reply the woman in the green dress ceased to gaze at the sky and obviously decided to get this dog show over as quickly as possible. With a smile that would freeze a volcano, she took the hailer from the other woman and spoke into it. "Now that my companion, with whom I share this platform, has managed to achieve some degree of organisation to this event, which I must say is quite unlike any other that I have experienced, let us proceed without delay."

If the larger woman had a voice that commanded instant obedience, the other woman had a voice that was so high-pitched and nasal that it caused one's ears to vibrate. "Are you two and that dog coming in or are you not?"

The entire assembly, human and dog, turned and stared at Spike and the Professor. The Professor felt himself starting to blush. Spike wished the ground would open up and swallow him. But it was Brandy who seemed to be most affected by the second woman's voice. No longer like a statue, he started to tremble and quiver. He also started to move, obliging the Professor and Spike to follow instead of having to lead him.

"Ah now that's better," the second woman said. "Which section…?"

But Brandy had no interest in sections. He was interested only in the source of the voice that had released him from the state of shock he had experienced at seeing so many of his own kind at the one time.

"Whoa!" The Professor tugged at the clothes line but Brandy's determination had given him a new-found strength. As he reached the first group of household pets, he bounded forward into the middle of them. The clothes line snapped where it was tied to his collar. The Professor stared unbelievingly at the dogless cord in his hand. But Brandy went on, oblivious of the terror and outrage he caused among the hitherto tranquil canines and their handlers.

The tweedy lady snatched the hailer back as dogs and young people scattered out of Brandy's way. "If the owners of this brute do not control him at once..."

The pandemonium in the pets' section was having a knock-on effect in the special breed category. Brandy's boldness seemed to strike a sympathetic response in animals unused to being made lie in a state of quietness. They rose to their feet and opened their mouths and yelled with such fierceness that even the young people who owned them, as opposed to simply having borrowed them for the occasion, felt control slip away from them.

Brandy reached the platform and launched himself on the woman in green who screamed loudly as Brandy knocked her hat off and began to lick her face.

Spike and the Professor scrambled through the tangle of leads and snarling, snapping dogs and yelling and tearful young people.

"Cats," Spike yelled. "Where's the cat?"

But instead of distracting Brandy from his task of thanking the woman, Spike's words further increased the chaos as dogs all over the place responded to his call.

A kind of demented chase was now taking place with dogs being pursued by their controllers through the flowerbeds and around the seats where grown-ups, who had gathered to watch the contest, either yelled in fright or roared with laughter.

Spike and the Professor had reached the platform by now. The tweedy woman's eyes had glazed over and she kept making unsuccessful attempts to raise the hailer to her lips.

The Professor wondered if a different voice might have a positive effect on the situation. "Excuse me," he said and took the hailer from the woman. He put it to his mouth and yelled "QUIET-T-T."

The word bounced around the Green, rattled the glass in a newspaper shop and brought everything to an abrupt halt. "Now, Brandy," he said to the dog who had been startled into leaving the second judge alone. "Come here, Brandy…"

Too late he remembered that he still had the hailer in his hand and had spoken into it. The effect of hearing his name spoken so deafeningly caused yet another change in Brandy's mood. He went back to being deeply suspicious of Spike and the Professor. When they tried to take hold of his collar, he bolted for the railings, slipped through them and vanished up Newgrove Avenue.

"That leads to the Strand Road," Spike shouted. "He could be killed if he tries to run across the road. Come on!"

Spike sprinted through he crowd, most of which had managed, thanks to the Professor's shout, to grab hold of their animals. The few dogs on the loose were chasing each other around a chestnut tree.

The Professor handed the hailer to the woman in tweeds. "Thanks very much for the …"

Then he saw the expression in her eyes and decided not to say anything else. When he looked back from the main gate into the Green, the second woman had begun to argue with her companion, who refused to heed what was being said to her and instead once more lifted the hailer to her lips. "The competition will continue as arranged. I will not allow this deliberate attempt at sabotage..."

Sabotage! The woman in tweeds thought he and Spike had deliberately tried to sabotage the show! And Doreen was still there, listening!

"Once more to my left, the household pets, to my right the special breeds. And be quick about it."

Chapter Seven

randy, for one moment, hesitated about which direction to take; down Durham Road or straight on towards Strand Road.

"Let him find the smells on Durham Road, great," Spike intoned as he put on an extra spurt but Brandy wasn't the kind of dog to take the wishes of a mere boy into consideration, even if that boy was one of the pair who had released him into this amazing world of total fear, total delight and total liberty. So he rejected Durham Road and exercised his new-found right of choice to head for the strand which his nose told him was just beyond the low wall at the next intersection.

Spike called, "No, Brandy! No, Brandy! Wait! Wait!"

But the dog ran on and dashed across the

road just as there was a major break in traffic caused by a train using the level crossing at Merrion Gates and the lights at the end of Beach Road turning red.

The Professor caught up with Spike. "The judges think we did it all deliberately. Doreen heard what was said…"

The two boys ran to the strand wall and looked over it. Brandy was headed towards Dun Laoghaire pier and the open sea.

"Thank heavens the tide is out," the Professor said, as he and Spike ran down a flight of steps.

"He might be easier to catch if it was in," Spike said.

"He might drown."

"Dogs can swim."

"Only if they've sense enough to try," the Professor replied.

And Brandy had shown almost no sense so far. Now that he'd started to run, would he simply continue to run until he could run no further?

"We'll never catch him," Spike said.

"We have to catch him or at least see what happens to him," the Professor declared. "He's our responsibility now. We'd get into terrible trouble if we just left him."

"We couldn't be in worse trouble than we are already," Spike replied. "Dozens of people at the dog show know who we are. They might know whose dog Brandy is. We've probably broken at least a dozen laws. And who'll believe it wasn't deliberate? All those other kids who were there hate us, especially the ones that don't win."

"We can't think of ourselves now," panted the Professor. "We have to prevent Brandy from galloping into the sea and maybe drowning."

"He's stopped," Spike said.

And indeed Brandy had stopped and once more had become like a statue.

"We'll have to creep up on him," the Professor said "Any sudden noise will start him off again."

"But there's terrible slimy seaweed all around us."

"That can't be helped," said the Professor. "It's our duty."

Reluctantly Spike got down on his hands and knees and began to crawl towards Brandy. The Professor went even further by crawling on his stomach, signalling to Spike that he would approach the dog from the other side."It's what they call a pincer movement,"

Spike told himself reassuringly. And he needed reassurance for it occurred to him that the space between himself and the Professor was now so large that Brandy could simply run between or around them. Or worse, take off again and leave the two boys feeling very silly, very dirty and also very, very smelly, for the seaweed was throwing off a worse stench then his granny's hatbox or the burnt butter.

Suddenly Brandy quivered like he had in the back garden of the mews and at the entrance to Sandymount Green. Only there now seemed to be no reason for another attack of nerves. He dropped down on his stomach and began to crawl forward almost as though he was imitating the Professor.

Then, as if released from a catapult, the dog sprang forward. At once, a huge flock of seabirds, that had been resting out of sight behind a sandbank, rose up, wheeling and whirling and screaming in alarm and indignation. They turned in an arc and passed over the boys' heads with Brandy, neck out-stretched, in useless pursuit and too occupied to notice how close he was to the Professor.

The Professor timed his move perfectly and, like a rugby player, tackled Brandy and held on firmly in spite of Brandy's determination to continue his pursuit of the birds. Spike secured the clothes line once again to the dog's collar.

The seabirds were now so far away as to seem like pieces of paper scattered high in the sky. Brandy accepted that the chase was over and, at the same time, recovered from his disappointment in the delight of realising who it was who had interrupted his activity.

"You'd think he hadn't seen us for years and years instead of just a few minutes," declared Spike as he fended off the dog's attempt to lick his face. "I've never known a dog to be so fond of licking."

"Or so dirty a dog," moaned the Professor. "He's covered in seaweed and sand. And we're not much better."

They were in fact worse, with great green stains on their clothes and the foul smell of the seaweed on their hands and hair and faces.

"Not only can we not go home like this, but we can't possibly leave Brandy back in Miss Finucane's without washing him. She'd call the guards." The Professor looked down at Brandy who wagged his tail and suddenly seemed content to behave like any normal, well-trained dog.

"I don't suppose there's any chance of giving him a bath at your house," said Spike.

"No. He might bark if we took him there. My mother would hear him even if she didn't smell us. Brandy's calm enough now because he's got used to us and to being on the strand. What about your granny's? Could we not wash Brandy and ourselves there? I mean we wouldn't need to have a bath. And maybe the seaweed stains will dry and we'd be able to brush them off. We won't be expected home for almost three hours."

Three hours? It didn't seem possible to Spike that it was only the middle of the afternoon; and the middle of the afternoon of the same day.

The two boys, with Brandy at their heels, headed for the mound with its three great chimneys. Howth Head sparkled in the sunlight. Yachts skimmed across the bay, their sails filled with the fresh south-easterly breeze that had blown away any trace of cloud. A great white ship sailed out from the Alexandra Basin.

"That's what I wish I was on," declared Spike, "headed for somewhere hundreds of miles away, like Spain."

"We're in trouble enough trying to get as far as Cork," the Professor replied. "Think of the mess we'd be in if we attempted to cross the ocean."

Chapter Eight

very path, every short-cut on the mound had either a group of children or mothers pushing prams or adults walking dogs along it. And everyone had had a question to ask or a remark to pass on the state of Brandy and the boys.

At first Spike had tried to give the impression that nothing of any importance had happened until finally the Professor said, "You're only making things worse. Just pretend you haven't heard the question."

And so, like two green-stained zombies, they had hurried along in silence until they reached the safety of Granny O'Brien's house.

They paused for a second to recover from the experiences of the day.

Brandy flopped down on the linoleum in the kitchen.

"He needs a drink of water," Spike said.

"We'll wash him first."

"We'd better do it down here then. We don't want to trail dirt upstairs. There's an old bath hanging behind the back door."

"Bring in some newspapers as well to put on the floor. Only this time, make sure there's no coal dust on them."

Brandy watched with great interest as the boys covered the area around him with newspaper. He sniffed at the old metal bath. It seemed harmless enough but then who was to know what excitement could come out of the most innocent occurrence? His two companions must be the most interesting humans a dog could hope to meet.

"We'll use a saucepan to fill the bath," the Professor said.

Fortunately, there seemed to be plenty of hot water and the boys took turns to empty saucepans of it into the bath.

When the bath was almost half full, the Professor tested the water by dipping his finger in it. "We might scare him if we put him in there. We'll add some cold."

When the water was running really cold, the boys added four saucepans of it into the bath.

"That seems just about right now," the Professor said, having once more dipped his finger. "Now we'll have to go about this very carefully so as not to panic Brandy and maybe upset the bath. Here, Brandy! Nice Brandy! Who's going to be a nice clean dog?"

Brandy twisted his head to one side. The only sound he recognised for sure was his own name.

"Nice water just for Brandy." Spike sprinkled a few drops of water on Brandy's front paw.

The dog sniffed at his paw and seemed not to be upset.

The Professor sprinkled a few drops on Brandy's head.

Brandy shook his head playfully. His tail began to wag.

"I think he might like water," Spike said. "Why don't we dip his other paw in it?"

Brandy obligingly allowed his paw to be placed in it.

Then he allowed his other front paw to be placed in it.

He waited with interest to see what might happen next. And for a second almost began to quiver when the boys lifted him up and sat him in the water, which came up to his chest.

But the water was really quite pleasant. Even when the boys began to pour saucepans of it over him, he didn't mind too much. It was certainly less frightening then being dumped in Miss Finucane's big bath and having the shower turned full on him. Also the soap that Spike used didn't go all bubbly.

"I think this is going to be easier than we thought," said the Professor but he touched the leg of the kitchen table 'for good luck' just in case. "Is there a towel we can use? It can go into the washing machine at my house. Mother'll never notice it."

Spike brought down the largest towel that he could find. They lifted Brandy carefully out of the bath and began to dry him. He raised no objection at all and, as soon as they released him, he gave them both a well-controlled lick and slumped under the kitchen table where he began to examine his coat for any traces of sand or seaweed.

Spike and the Professor lifted the bath off the floor and managed to empty it into the sink without spilling too much of it. The water was dark grey with dirt.

"I think we actually did Miss Finucane a favour by taking Brandy out this afternoon," the Professor said. "He's probably never had so much fun or been so clean."

"Or caused so much trouble." Suddenly Spike began to grin. "Do you remember the look on your woman's face when he came charging towards the platform?"

"Or the way so many of the other dogs went berserk when they heard the word 'cat'." The Professor was laughing as well. "Do you think they actually know what the word means? I mean when you say the word to a dog, does he actually see a cat in his mind's eye?"

"Be careful. He's listening." Spike nodded in the direction of Brandy who had suspended the examining of his coat to see if the word "cat" would prove to be start of a new outing.

"Still, he's not a bad old brute. Hand me the towel and I'll dry the inside of the bath. Then no-one will ever know it's been used."

Spike paused in the action of handling the towel to the Professor. "What is that?"

The Professor looked out the window. The backyard was almost completely obscured by white foam.

"I don't know. It's like suds of some kind."

"But where is it coming from?" As Spike leaned forward to get a better view, the door into the lane opened and Doreen came in.

She stared in horror at the suds. Then

seeing Spike and the Professor at the window,
she rushed into the house before Spike had
time to lock the back door.

"What's going on here? Why is the back door
and the lane door unlocked?"

"We went out that way earlier on," the
Professor said.

"So in other words, anyone could have
walked in here..."

"We just forgot and anyway no-one did walk
in," Spike said.

"No, but they might come in now that you're
filling the whole place with bubbles."

"The bubbles have nothing to do with us,"
said the Professor.

"Well, they're coming out of the drain in the
yard and there's no-one in here except the two
of you. And that mad dog," she added, noticing
Brandy under the table. "There's probably a
warrant out for his arrest."

"You can't arrest a dog," the Professor said.
"Isn't that right, Spike?"

"Washing powder," Spike replied. "It's the
washing powder."

"We used soap, not washing powder," said
the Professor.

"The stuff we spilled when we broke the
cupboard door. I put it down the sink. The

rush of bath water all at once was too great, so it's bubbling up out of the drain. The breeze is blowing it all over the place."

"There'll be grown-ups around here before you know what's happened," warned Doreen. "All the neighbours know that Granny is away." She cast an eye around the kitchen. "The cupboard isn't the only damage you did by the look of things. I might be able to help but only if you tell me what you've been up to."

Doreen's eyes grew wider and wider with every word that she heard. "Well aren't you the two right eejits," she said when they'd finished. "But let's start with what's easiest. That means getting rid of the bubbles." She rolled up the newspapers on the floor and carried them outside into the yard where she placed them over the top of the drain. The bubbles stopped at once although quite a few still floated in the air.

"They'll soon vanish," she declared. "Now you can get to work on the table."

The two boys looked at the table. It was covered with the remains of their sandwich making: crusts, crumbs, smears of margarine, bits of ham fat, squashed tomatoes; all quite disgusting-looking.

"Come on," Doreen ordered, " and get a bag

to put the bits in. Then wash the table."

There was a loud knocking at the front door.

"I'll go," Doreen said.

The Professor put his arms around Brandy to prevent him from barking. Spike leaned against the closed kitchen door and listened but he could only distinguish the voice of the caller as a different sound to Doreen's.

The front door was closed.

Doreen came back into the kitchen. "That was Mrs Moody," she announced. "She was enquiring about how you were since Spike fell into the trench."

Spike moaned. "Granny's friend. The woman we met on our way back from Baggot Street Bridge."

"She called at our house first but Mam and Dad were both out. She wanted to know where the bubbles were coming from. Apparently you can see them from the street."

"What did you tell her?"

"I told her that the wind blew them up that high."

The Professor was amazed. "And that answer satisfied her?"

"Well she went away, didn't she? Mind you, I think she might come back. The sooner we get finished in here the better."

Spike and the Professor

The boys worked as quickly as possible on the table, scraping off the remains of the food and then washing it down several times with soap and hot water. Doreen turned her attention to the oven, managing to get the burnt butter off it and then placing the broken dish on the draining board. "What about the door on the cupboard?" she asked, stooping down to examine it. "It's just popped out of its hinges. It's just a matter of pushing it back into place. There we are." She surveyed the kitchen. "This place looks more or less all right now."

"I'll take the towel home and wash it," the Professor said.

"And I'll take the papers off the drain later on," Spike added.

"Did either of you go upstairs? I mean, touch anything upstairs?"

"Only for the towel," Spike said. "Oh, I nearly forgot about the hatbox." Spike retrieved the box from where it lay in a corner of the yard. It smelled as bad as ever and looked much the worse for wear. "I don't think I should bring it into the house."

"I agree," said Doreen. "It's like manure of some kind."

"Of course," nodded the Professor. "The man

that shouted at us out the window must have been going to fix up the front garden and had put the manure out of the way under the hedge. Could we not wash the box?"

"And how could you dry it without it falling to bits?" Doreen asked.

Spike shrugged hopelessly. "What's the point of worrying about an old hatbox when there's the plate and the pram and all that other stuff?"

"What's to stop you from trying to get the plate back?" asked Doreen. "And the pram as well?"

"Doreen is right," declared the Professor. "We're being negative at a time when we should be positive. We should fix what we can fix and maybe we can fix the pram like we did the cupboard door. Or get someone to fix it."

"And maybe I can help you over the hatbox," Doreen said. "Granny gave me one very like it to keep my 'Fab Girl' comics in. She might never notice the difference if we swapped the boxes around."

"And you'd do that to help us, would you?" asked Spike.

"Yes, but only this once," Doreen said. "And it's as much for Granny's sake as yours. I don't want her to think that she can't go away for a visit without having her house wrecked. I'll go and get the other box while you bring that wild animal back where he belongs."

The wild animal was by now almost dry and had greatly enjoyed lying under the table listening to the conversation. He was even more delighted when the Professor tied the clothes line back onto his collar. He went and sat at the back door as though he'd lived in Granny O'Brien's house for years and years.

"We'll take the quickest way," declared the Professor. "There'd be no point in trying to hide now."

"What about our clothes?" asked Spike. "Washing Brandy seems to have got most of the slime off our hands and faces." He touched his shirt. "But this is still wet and pongs as much as ever."

"I can get you clean clothes when I go for the box," said Doreen, "but I don't know what I can do about the Professor."

"Could you lend him a pair of your own jeans and a teeshirt?" asked Spike. "You're about the same size."

Both Doreen and the Professor were about to object to this plan: the professor because he didn't want to go around in Doreen's clothes, Doreen because she didn't care for the idea of lending her clothes to anyone.

"It'd only be for an hour or so," Spike said, "and it's not as though I was asking the Professor to put on a dress."

"Well all right," Doreen agreed reluctantly, "but not until you are back here with the plate and the pram. I don't want to take a chance on you doing anything messy while he's wearing my things."

"O.K. We'll be as quick as we can," Spike said.

"Leave the front door key with me. You go out the back. That way I can lock up after you."

When they were safely away from his granny's house, Spike said, "I never thought we'd end up depending on Doreen."

"I never thought we'd end up depending on anyone," retorted the Professor. "It all seemed so easy this morning. Now the only person to have got anything out of it is Brandy."

Brandy wagged his tail and looked over the sea wall at the incoming tide.

"We might be better on the other side of the road in case he decided to try and go after the seabirds again," said Spike.

Brandy seemed just as happy walking along by the garden walls. Rush-hour traffic was just starting. It shielded him and the two boys from the line of strollers enjoying the bright sunshine. Spike caught sight of his parents, arm in arm, walking back towards Irishtown. Fortunately, an enormous lorry, bound for the ferry, passed almost immediately and so Mr and Mrs O'Halligan did not see their son. And, relieved as he was, Spike knew in his heart that sooner or later, his luck would run out. There had been too many narrow escapes.

Chapter Nine

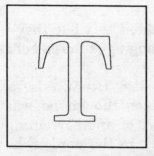

he problem was getting
Brandy back into Miss
Finucane's garden.

There was no shed for the boys to stand on,
on the side of the garden wall they now faced.
Spike could give the Professor a leg up but
he'd never manage to lift Brandy up to him
anymore than the Professor could be expected
to manage to take such a heavy dog from him.

"We could have a terrible accident," said
Spike. "And if we try hauling him up by the
clothes line, we might strangle him."

"We'll just have to find something to stand
on," the Professor said.

"Such as what?" asked Spike.

"Back there a bit," the Professor said, "did
we not pass a barrel that was never taken
away when they finished mending the road
last year? Would we not be able to roll that up

as far as here and stand on that? You could get up on the wall first and I'd easily manage to pass Brandy to you."

"What'll people say if they see us rolling a barrel along?"

"It'd be nothing compared to what they'd say if they saw Brandy hanging at the end of a clothes line. Come on."

Brandy regarded the last two words as applying to him and, even though he was surprised at the prospect of another outing instead of being left back in the garden, he was delighted at the idea. But then, he heard a key turn in the garden gate lock.

Spike and the Professor automatically jumped back and looked for somewhere to hide. But there was nowhere for them to go. They would just have to face Miss Finucane and confess that they had taken Brandy without her permission. But it wasn't Miss Finucane who came out of the garden. It was a man that neither of the boys had ever seen before. He was carrying a large nylon holdhall. He was very startled when he saw Spike and the Professor. He looked even more alarmed when he saw Brandy. He began to walk very quickly away from the three of them. Whatever was in the holdall was

obviously quite heavy to judge from the way
that the man leaned to one side.

"Who's that?" asked Spike.

"I don't know." The Professor ran to the
open garden door and looked inside. The patio
doors were wide open. "Miss Finucane?"

There was no reply.

The Professor called her name even more
loudly. "Miss Finucane?"

There was still no reply.

The Professor shouted to Spike. "I think
that man is a burglar. I think he's just robbed
Miss Finucane's house."

Spike, with Brandy at his heels, took off
after the man. "Hey, you! Stop! Stop or I'll set
the dog on you!"

The man gave a terrified look over his
shoulder. Spike made as if to release his grip
on the clothes line. "O.K., Brandy. Go get
him!"

Brandy obligingly made as if to spring
forward. The man dropped the holdall and ran
as if his life depended on it.

"You keep hold of Brandy. I'll see where he's
gone to." The Professor dashed past Spike and
arrived at the next corner in time to see the
man get into a waiting car and be driven off.
The Professor memorised the registration

number of the vehicle and ran back to Spike.

Spike was opening the holdall. "It's full of bits of silver and jewellery," he said. "What do we do now?"

"Tell the guards. You and Brandy go back and wait by the door. I can use the telephone in my house."

Mrs O'Neill heard the side door slam and, in spite of being half way through the writing of her book review, could not fail to notice that there was something very odd about the look and smell of her son. "What on…"

"There's been a burglary."

"A what…?"

The Professor grabbed a piece of paper and wrote down the number of the get-away car before he forgot it. "Around at Miss Finucane's. Spike and I almost caught him."

Mrs O'Neill flicked open the telephone pad beside her and dialled Irishtown Garda Station, giving the details as she had got them from the Professor. "Yes, that's right. My son and his friend." She listened briefly. "Yes, of course." She replaced the receiver. "They'll send the squad car at once. They'll want to talk to you and Spike." She glanced sadly at her typewriter. Then she said, "It'll just have to wait. I'm coming with you. Go and make sure that the front door and the door into the garage are all locked. If they can get into Miss Finucane's, they can get in anywhere."

"Miss Finucane's is very easy to burgle," the Professor said. "All you have to do is to climb over the garden wall."

"But she has the great big dog and a burglar alarm." Mrs O'Neill turned the key in the side entrance and led the way down the path. "In fact, did you not say something to me earlier on about talking the dog for a walk?"

"Yes…"

"But of course Miss Finucane wouldn't have been home. The burglar must have known that as well." She moved slightly away from the Professor. "What is that terrible smell?"

"Seaweed," the Professor said, apologetically. "Spike and I were on the strand."

"You must have crawled along it to get into that state."

The Professor smiled weakly but his mother did not continue the conversation for they were almost at Miss Finucane's back garden gate now. Spike was standing there with Brandy, greatly refreshed by a drink of water from his bowl, lying beside him. The clothes line, neatly rolled up, was back in its place.

Almost at once the squad car arrived. Out of it got the same two guards who had been at the scene of the accident in Londonbridge Road. Neither of them remembered the Professor from that day. Both were very business-like in their questions.

"You saw this man come out of the back gate with this bag in his hand?"

"Yes."

"When he realised that you were following him, he dropped the bag and ran?"

"Yes."

"Can you describe him?"

The boys did. Their descriptions matched exactly.

"And I have the number of the car that took him away." The Professor handed over the piece of paper. "I couldn't see who was driving it."

"It'll probably have been stolen," one of the guards said. "Thieves seldom use their own cars when they're out on a job. But the description you've given us is a great help. We'd like you to come down to the station and make a statement later on."

The boys nodded.

"What about the house here?" Mrs O'Neill asked. "Miss Finucane won't be home for almost an hour."

"We'll get in touch with her now. And someone from the detective bureau will be along
soon as well to check for fingerprints."

"How could anyone get into the house with a
burglar alarm on?" the professor asked.

"Maybe the alarm wasn't on," said the
guard.

"But how would the burglar know that?"

"He wouldn't until he tried to open,
probably in this case, the front door."

"But he had a key of the back gate. It's still
in the lock."

"You'd be surprised at the foolish things
some people do. I'd almost bet that the owner
of the house left the back door key in the lock
and the key to the back gate hanging on a hook
close by. It happens all the time."

"But how would the burglar know the house
was empty?"

Suddenly Spike realised why the Professor
was asking so many questions. He wanted to
make quite sure that the burglar hadn't seen
the two of them climbing in and out of the back
garden with Brandy and had known from that
that the house was empty.

The guard said, "I think you'll find that the
people who live in these houses are out all day

every day, Monday to Friday. By keeping an eye on the place, criminals would soon get to know people's movements."

"So if anyone was to come and, say, borrow a dog, they couldn't be blamed for anything else that happened?" the Professor asked.

"Borrow a dog?" The guards exchanged glances. Their eyes began to twinkle. "On the contrary, I'd say they might have saved the dog from being hurt, especially if the dog was a friendly as this one, although you can't always tell with dogs."

"That's right," said the second guard. "There was a report this afternoon of a riot in the Green. It seems an entry in the dog show went crazy."

The Professor felt himself beginning to blush.

"The question, of course, is—was that riot started deliberately!" observed the first guard.

"Oh no," the Professor said quickly. "It was all an accident. I...I mean, who'd want to start a riot at a dog show especially if they wanted to win first prize?"

"That's true enough. Well, we'd best get on with things. Is there any chance you could take that dog with you? In case he gets into the house here and destroys clues before the detectives arrive?"

"Don't worry. We'll look after Brandy," Mrs O'Neill said.

The guards locked the back gate, taking the keys with them. After they'd driven away, Mrs O'Neill turned her attention to Spike and the Professor. "And what exactly was all that about riots and dog shows and borrowing dogs?"

"We climbed over the wall," said the Professor. "We borrowed Brandy."

"And supposing you'd been seen? Worse, supposing you were seen after the burglary, just think of all the trouble you could be in now!"

"We were trying to get the money for the outing to Cork and Kinsale," said Spike. "Or maybe I should say that the Professor was trying to help me get the money."

"The Professor? Is that what you call him? Is that his nickname?"

Spike nodded.

"Well, Professor," Mrs O'Neill said to her son. "It's about time you started using your brains. You can start by coming home to wash and change your clothes."

"Oh, but we've fixed to borrow some for Doreen. She's my sister." Spike had spoken without thinking.

"Well, I don't think we need avail ourselves of Doreen's offer," Mrs O'Neill said rather firmly. "Now I'll walk on back slowly with Brandy. I have a feeling that the poor brute has had enough excitement for one day. The Professor will go straight home, change his clothes, leave the dirty ones in the laundry basket and stay out of all trouble for the rest of not only today but, in so far as is possible, every day yet to come. All right?"

The two boys nodded and didn't speak until they were well out of earshot of Mrs O'Neill. "It could all come out now," said Spike, "the pram, the sandwiches, the dog show, everything."

"The main thing is that no-one seems to want to blame us for the burglary," said the Professor. "In fact, in a way you could say we saved Miss Finucane's silver and jewellery and were also a great help to the guards. I don't think they'll ask any more questions about the dog show. Why don't you and I collect the pram and see if you can find the dish as well?"

Chapter Ten

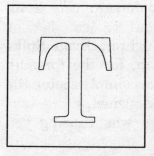

he workmen were packing up, anxious to get back to the depot before the rush hour traffic began in earnest. And with the rush hour, when there would be usual abuse from drivers who saw the roadworks as a deliberate attempt on the part of Dublin Corporation to make the trip home as long and as difficult as possible.

The pram was more or less as when Spike had last seen it, in a heap against the hut.

The foreman nudged the workman next to him. "Hey look, it's Ben Hur of the ham sandwiches. Had any good accidents since we last met?"

"No," said Spike.

"Well, you certainly look as though you've been up to or, maybe I should say, into something. 'Ben Hur meets the Green Stain.'

It'll probably be on television next week."

All the workmen joined in the general merriment caused by the foreman's remarks.

"Incidentally, we won't be needing any sandwiches for lunch tomorrow. We're all going on a diet."

That caused more laughter. Even Spike found it hard not to grin, for the foreman wasn't being nasty. He was simply seeing the funny side of what had happened.

"Did that woman who was chasing you catch up with you?"

"Mrs Moody..."

"Mrs Moody?" The foreman laughed some more. "Well she was certainly good and moody when she left here."

"What did you tell her?" asked Spike.

"Nothing. What could we tell her? And she was too interested in keeping up with you and your pal. Where's he anyway?"

"At home. I've come for the pram..."

"And the family heirloom, no doubt." The foreman went into the hut and carried out Granny's dish, sparkling clean and not as much as the tiniest crack. "It didn't break because of the mud. And the pram might not be too bad either. The reason it fell to bits is because it was so old and probably hadn't been used for ages. Your best bet would be to get some wire to put it back together. That way it'll be better than ever. You'll have done whoever it belongs to a great favour."

"Except that I haven't any wire with me," Spike said.

"You can leave it in the hut until tomorrow. Come back with your friend and do it then. Come at dinner-time and we'll give you a hand. Only promise us all, no sandwiches!"

The foreman helped Spike store the pram in the hut and locked the door. "See you tomorrow then, ould son. And remember every cloud has a silver lining." He got in beside the driver, and with a great hooting of the horn and whistles and cheers, the workmen were taken off in the direction of the city centre.

Spike stood quite still for a few seconds, holding the dish against his chest and considered how less hopeless the situation had become. Brandy was clean and safe. So were Miss Finucane's belongings. His granny's house was more or less as it should be. The pram would actually be improved on. There was only the question of buying the food that he and the Professor had used for the sandwiches.

Maybe later on he and the Professor could tell everyone the whole story. Maybe in fact they'd better do that before Mrs Moody came around to call again.

Doreen opened the front door of Granny O'Brien's before Spike even had time to knock. The Professor, dressed in clean clothes, was in the hall. "That was quick," Spike said.

"You got the dish?"

"Yes."

"Put it back where you found it before something happens to it," advised Doreen. "Your clean clothes are upstairs. I put Granny's hats in my box. She'll never know the difference."

"I think maybe we should tell her all the same," Spike said. The Professor and I have to buy food that we borrowed from her fridge as well!"

"That means no day-trip then," Doreen said.

"You'll still be able to go."

"By myself? I haven't enough money to take anyone else."

"Who won the dog show then?"

"A cocker spaniel from Ballsbridge and Archie Lynch's dog, Sprat."

"That old mongrel? I don't believe you," Spike said as he went upstairs.

Doreen checked the yard one last time. The newspapers from the drain she'd put at the bottom of the bin. All signs of the bubbles had vanished and the overflow of detergent from the drain had left the yard looking very, very clean.

The same could be said of the kitchen floor where the wet newspapers and Brandy had lain. The kitchen table was as white as snow.

The Professor put the still-damp towel into the carrier bag that Doreen had used for the changes of clothes. "I'll bring it back tomorrow morning."

"O.K."

Spike came down with his green-stained clothes under his arm.

"I'll take those with me too," said the Professor. "Mother won't mind."

Doreen carefully locked all the doors and the back gate. For the first time since early morning, Spike and the Professor had nothing to do, nowhere to rush off to. "I'll walk back with you to your place and see how Brandy is getting on," Spike said.

"All right. You're welcome to come with us if you want, Doreen."

"We should call into Sandymount Green and see if there are any competitions on tomorrow," Doreen suggested.

"I think I've had enough competitions for the moment," Spike said.

"That's stupid," said Doreen. "Supposing it was for something you and the Professor were good at, like..." Doreen thought for a second and said, "Well, you could at least look."

"I think we'd be better staying away from the Green for the moment" said the Professor. "People might still be very cross about the dog show."

"Then I'll catch up with you in a few minutes." Doreen cut down Seafort Avenue.

Traffic was solid now on Strand Road, the smell of exhaust fumes mingling with the smell of the tide.

"Actually," said the Professor, "just because we can't go to Cork doesn't mean we can't go somewhere else."

"Like where?"

"Like somewhere on the Dart."

DART stood for Dublin Area Rapid Transport. Every fifteen to twenty minutes, trains went from one side of Dublin Bay to the other.

"It'd certainly be cheaper than the day

excursion to Cork."

"Of course it would. We could go to Killiney. I hear there's a rock on the hill there in the shape of an eagle."

"And there's supposed to be a racehorse buried there as well."

"I wonder if it died when it fell into a trench," joked the Professor.

"Eejit," said Spike.

"No," said the Professor. "Last home to my house is the eejit."

The two boys raced along, totally unaware of the many envious glances they got from the drivers in the many different vehicles. They crossed the road at the Tower, went down St John's Road and, within minutes, neck and neck, collapsed into the back garden. Brandy, with a great woof of delight, hurled himself out of the shade of the shrubbery and landed on top of them. The three of them rolled around mindlessly happy on the grass. Then Brandy broke away at the sound of voices in the house. The two boys sat up. Miss Finucane and Mrs O'Neill stepped out onto the patio. Brandy ran towards them but much more quietly than the way he had greeted the boys.

"Hello, Brandy." Miss Finucane gently

patted the dog's head. "I hear you've had quite a day." She smiled at Spike and the Professor. "And I understand that I have very good reason to be grateful to the two of you for saving me from my own stupidity."

"You didn't turn on the alarm then?" Spike said.

"No. I didn't. I was late this morning and just forgot. But now I hope you will let me show my appreciation for what you've done in a more practical way..."

"I think perhaps, before you say anything else, that the two boys might have something to tell you about how they came to be at your house," Mrs O'Neill said.

"We borrowed Brandy for the dog show," the Professor said. "We climbed over your wall and got him out that way. We were bringing him back when we met the burglar."

"Heavens," said Miss Finucane, "and did Brandy win?"

"No. He got a bit over-excited."

"Well, that's the best news I've heard all day."

"Do you mean about him being over-excited?" asked Spike.

"Yes," said Miss Finucane. "I was quite worried about him being too quiet, almost depressed. I suppose it's because he's by himself all day and never sees other dogs."

"We'd take him out for you if you like," said the Professor.

"Would you really?"

"Yes. All you need do is give us a key of the back gate."

"Well, that would be ideal. But first things first." Miss Finucane started to open her handbag. Mrs O'Neill put out a restraining hand. "Just a moment, please, Miss Finucane. I don't think the boys expect a reward. I'm not even sure that they deserve a reward."

"Oh but surely..."

"I think Mother means that we might have been the cause of the burglary. If we were seen climbing over the wall..."

"I would have thought that, if the burglar had seen you and Spike climbing over the wall, he wouldn't have gone near the place in case it had already been broken into."

"We can't be a hundred percent certain of that," said Mrs O'Neill.

"That's true," nodded the Professor. "And if Brandy had been in the back garden, he might have frightened the burglar."

"Do you really think so?" Miss Finucane looked down at Brandy, who had flopped

down at her feet like a rolled-up rug. "Well
then, if you feel that a reward isn't right,
there is the question of payment for walking
Brandy. No, now I insist. It would be a great
help to me. And, of course, to Brandy as well.
Five walks a week, one pound a walk.
Payment one week in advance." Miss
Finucane took a five-pound note out of her
purse. That left the boys only one pound and
sixty-five pence short for Granny's food. And
with a regular income of five pounds a week,
they might have enough to go on another day
trip before the end of the summer holidays.
"Who's going to take charge of the money?"

"Spike will," said the Professor. "And thank
you very much."

"Yes, Miss Finucane. Thanks very much."
Spike put the five-pound note in his back
pocket and suddenly noticed that his clean
jeans were streaked with green from rolling
on the grass. So were the Professor's. If they
weren't careful, they'd run out of clean
clothes. But a bit of green didn't matter now
that they could replace the food.

"Miss Finucane and I are going to have
some tea. Would you, boys, like that? Or
would you prefer some homemade lemonade?"

"Lemonade," they said together.

"Hello. Here comes Spike's sister."

Doreen opened the side gate. "Hello, Mrs O'Neill," she said.

"Hello. Doreen, isn't it?"

"Yes, Mrs O'Neill."

"The boys are going to have some lemonade. If you'd like some too you're more than welcome."

"Thanks, Mrs O'Neill."

"The Professor, as I suppose I'd better continue calling him, knows where the glasses are."

Miss Finucane and Mrs O'Neill went into the house. The boys made as if to follow. Doreen held them back. "What number were you in the dog show?"

"Don't tell us they're looking for us," Spike said.

"No, of course, they aren't. But what did you do with the number they gave you?"

"It must be in my jeans; they're in the carrier bag. But what difference..."

Doreen emptied the contents of the carrier bag onto the grass. She unrolled Spike's jeans and found the number in the back pocket. "I knew it must be yours. I just knew it. Twenty-seven." She looked at the boy's blank faces. "You won the raffle."

"What raffle?" the Professor asked.

"Everyone who entered in the dog show got the chance to enter a raffle. They put the result in the window just now. Number twenty-seven wins ten pounds!"

Ten pounds?

"But they'll never give it to us," Spike said, "not after what happened."

"The raffle has nothing to do with the dog show. The judges at the dog show will have gone home hours ago."

"But that means we nearly have enough for the excursion," said Spike.

"Of course it does," said Doreen.

The Professor remembered what his mother had said about all the tickets being sold. "Before we go down to the Green, I think we should telephone at once and reserve three tickets," he said. "We can use the telephone in the hall."

With hands slightly trembling, the Professor found the number in the directory and dialled it. It was answered at once. "Good afternoon. May I help you?"

"I'm enquiring about the day trip to Cork and Kinsale next week, please."

"Just one second. I'll put you through."

"There was a click. A different voice said.

"Hello, can I help you?"

"Yes. I'm enquiring about the day trip to Cork and Kinsale."

"For how many people, please?"

"Three people."

"Three adults?"

"No. Three under-fourteens…"

"Oh I'm sorry but under-fourteens have to be accompanied by at least one adult. Those are the rules, I'm afraid."

"Oh I see."

"Sorry again. Good-bye."

"Good-bye." The Professor hung up.

"What is it? What's wrong?"

"Under-fourteens have to be accompanied by an adult."

Spike slumped against the wall. "I don't believe it. Just as we almost had all the money. There's no chance of getting an adult to go with us."

"Not unless we could pay the full fare for whoever it was," said the Professor.

Mrs O'Neill carried a teatray out of the kitchen. "I thought you were going to have some lemonade."

"Yes, we will in a second."

Brandy came out of the sitting-room to see what the children were doing. His tail drooped as he sensed how sad they were.

"Best bring those clothes in from the garden," the Professor said. "We might as well drink the lemonade. My mouth is suddenly very dry."

"So is mine," said Spike.

They sat mournfully at the kitchen table. The lemonade tasted odd to Doreen but she didn't feel that was important enough to mention. She didn't even think it was important enough to have a good look at the kitchen. Instead as soon as she had finished her drink, she said, "We have to collect the prize money before the office closes."

The man who gave them the ten pounds, said, "You look more like people who've lost ten pounds instead of winning it."

"We just had a bit of a let-down, that's all," Doreen said. "But we really are delighted to have won the raffle, honestly we are."

Spike put the ten-pound note in his back pocket with the five-pound note. "Well now at least we have more than enough money for Granny's food."

"And a new butter dish, and a new teacloth," said Doreen.

Somehow, the butter dish and the teacloth had slipped the boys' minds. They wouldn't have been able to go on the excursion even if they hadn't needed an adult with them. "What do you think we should buy first?" asked Spike.

"The food," said Doreen, "in case Granny should come back early with the jockey. You'd better have the front door key again!"

Chapter Eleven

t was a good thing that the boy followed Doreen's advice because when they had bought the food they couldn't quite remember exactly the size of the butter dish. By the time they got the broken halves out of the bin, they arrived back to the shop in Ringsend just before closing time.

"I'm sorry," the owner said. "I've no more like that. You'd have to go to Lenehan's of Capel Street for a replacement. I sold the last one I had a week ago. I don't know when I'll have them in again."

Spike and the Professor weren't too upset to hear this. They'd easily get into the city centre first thing in the morning. "We might even buy the new dishcloth as well," the Professor said. "Then we can collect the pram. Your granny's bath towel should be ready to bring back as well."

"And Gran will understand if she finds out about the dish being broken," Spike remarked.

"Do you still intend to tell her the full story?"

"Yeh. Might as well get it out of the way. Then we won't have anything hanging over us. It's going to be great getting that money each week from Miss Finucane."

"Do you think we should save it all, maybe give it to your gran to hold on to for us?"

"Yeh. That's a great idea. Are you very disappointed about the trip to Cork?"

"Kind of. But, at the same time, I can't help thinking if we might not go one day by ourselves on just an ordinary bus. We could bring sandwiches. Have a kind of picnic. We wouldn't need an adult with us to do that, just our parents' permission. Your parents wouldn't mind, would they?"

"I don't know," Spike said.

"Do you mean they'd want us to take Doreen with us?"

"They might."

"Well that wouldn't matter. Doreen is all right."

"It's not really just Doreen. Maybe I should

think of spending any money I save on other things: things that I might need for school. We kind of rushed into the idea of the excursion. But now that it's definitely off, I've been thinking about Dad being out of work."

The Professor nodded understandingly. "Yeh. I see what you mean. But they wouldn't mind if you were to spend a bit of it on yourself."

"Oh they wouldn't say a word if I spent all of it on myself."

The day was starting to cool down. The blue of the sky was less bright. The spire of Ringsend Church threw a long shadow across the road. A group of weary adults and children trailed home from an afternoon spent on the promenade at Sandymount Strand. A number three bus crowded with more sunbaked people passed on its way into town. There was a sound of singing coming from the upstairs.

"Let's walk out and look at the yachts on the river," Spike said. "We have plenty of time before we have to go home to tea."

The two boys walked past the flats and the shops and pubs in Thorncastle Street. When they reached the place where the river Dodder and the river Liffey were definitely one river, they climbed over the wall and walked along the grass verge.

"This was the river once, you know," Spike said. "It got changed when they built the new road and the toll bridge."

"I wonder how things will be when we're grown up." The Professor looked at the buildings on the other side of the river. Once they had been warehouses for ships' cargoes. But now that ships no longer came that far up the river, they were being turned into offices and flats and conference centres like the Point where concerts were held as well.

"Gran sometimes says she was born in the age of the horse and cart and now she lives in the space age. We might see changes as great as that."

"Outer space laboratories? Holidays on Mars?"

"Yeh."

"My Dad thinks it could all be possible. He says that scientists think of space as the new frontier just like when America was discovered. People set off then not knowing for sure what they'd find."

The two boys sat on the wall and watched the traffic at the control points of the toll bridge. Drivers tossed money into baskets. Automatic barriers lifted and allowed vehicles to pass.

"Maybe no-one will have to work," the Professor said.

"My Dad wouldn't care for that. He's desperate because he hasn't got a job."

"Maybe it wouldn't matter so much if only a few people had jobs. But isn't that your father there?" The Professor pointed to a tall figure pushing a bicycle across the bridge. "I've never seen him with a bike before."

"Neither have I. He must have borrowed it from someone. Dad! Hey, Dad!"

Mr O'Halligan heard his son's voice above the hum of the traffic, turned and waved.

"Where are you going to?" Spike, followed by the Professor, scrambled towards the pedestrian crossing.

"I just got wind of a possible start."

"Do you mean a job?"

Mr O'Halligan nodded. "Yes. Only there's nothing settled. They're behind schedule with one of the riverside buildings so they're taking on an extra shift."

"When will you know?"

"Within the hour, but I mustn't delay. There'll be dozens after every vacancy." Mr O'Halligan got up on the bike and wobbled off.

"Whose bike is it?"

"Jack Byrne's," Mr O'Halligan yelled back. "See you at home."

Spike leaned against a railing and stared out to sea. "Wouldn't it be great if he did get a start? And I don't just mean so that I can spend my money."

"I know you don't mean that. Cripes, a whole hour to wait. What'll we do for a whole hour?"

"Nothing at all," said Spike.

"All the same, we don't want to hang around here. It might be hard for your Dad if . . . well, you know, if he had to tell us he didn't get the job. Come on back onto the strand."

They had gone less than a few hundred metres when they met Doreen. "Did you hear the news?" she asked.

"About the job. Yeh. We met Dad just now. You're not going to follow him, are you?"

"No, of course I'm not going to follow him. I'm going around to see my friend, Imelda."

It was news to Spike that Doreen and Imelda were friends. Imelda was very tall and very bossy, which didn't suit Doreen at all.

"What do you want to see her for?"

"I'm going to discuss an idea I have," Doreen replied in a deliberately mysterious way. "And that's all I can say for the moment."

The two boys looked at each other as Doreen walked off. "I'll bet she's thought of taking a bus to Cork as well," Spike said. "But she won't be let go without me. And I won't go at all if Imelda is going to be included in the outing."

"Neither will I," said the Professor. "United we stand, divided we fall."

"All for one and one for all." Spike flourished an imaginary sword above his head. Suddenly he and the Professor were in France at the time of The Three Musketeers. They gripped the reins of their imaginary steeds and galloped through Irishtown and out along Beach Road.

"Would it be wrong for me to offer you two gallants a lift?" Mr O'Neill, stalled in traffic, was laughing from his motor car. "I've something to talk to you about."

Spike and the Professor got into the car.

"How's the business of the outing going?"

"Well, we can't go on the special excursion. We thought maybe an ordinary bus."

"How would you like to drive down there with me? There's a meeting I have to attend on Tuesday. You'd have most of the day to yourselves. I'm not sure if you'll get as far as Kinsale."

"Oh that'd be great. Wouldn't it, Spike?"

"Yeh, terrific, although Brandy would have to miss his walk."

"Oh so you've become dog walkers now, have you?"

"Just one dog, Miss Finucane's."

"Well I'm sure she won't mind if you miss just one day." Traffic was moving again now.

"We might have to ask Doreen as well. She's Spike's sister."

"But not Imelda," declared Spike.

"No," the Professor agreed firmly, "not Imelda."

"Maybe," said Spike hopefully, "if Imelda can't come, Doreen won't either." He didn't really think that Doreen would refuse a free lift to Cork with or without Imelda, but so many other things were suddenly turning out so well, there was no harm in hoping.

"What's that you have there?" Mr O'Neill asked.

"Oh it's a broken butterdish," Spike said. "We're going to replace it in the morning."

"Then we have a broken pram to fix," the Professor said, "and a dishcloth to buy."

"You're having me on!" said Mr O'Neill.

"No, we're not," laughed the Professor. "It's a long story. But if you have the time , we have the inclination, as the Leaning Tower of Pisa once said to Big Ben."

"You should write all this down," Mr O'Neill said when the boys had finished, "keep a journal of the summer holidays."

"That's a great idea," the Professor said. "We could maybe enter for a competition."

"Indeed you could. Spike, are you not coming in to the house?"

"Oh no, thanks, Mr O'Neill. I think Mrs O'Neill has seen enough of me for one day."

"I'll call for you in the morning," the Professor said.

"O.K."

Spike hardly dared breathe, hardly dared hope as he walked back to Irishtown. Then he saw Doreen positively dancing with glee all be herself. Without being told, he knew that the news was good news. Dad had got a new start. The rest of the summer would be the best ever.

"Yahoo," he yelled. "Yahoo, Yahoo," and joined Doreen in her dance around the lamp post.

**Also by Tony Hickey
in Children's Poolbeg**

*Joe in the Middle
Where is Joe?*

*Spike and the Professor at the Races
Spike, the Professor and Doreen Go to London*

*Blanketland
Foodland
Legendland*

Children's
POOLBEG